Stories by M.T. Bass

Crossroads
In the Black
Lodging
Somethin' for Nothin'
Untethered
Article 15
Dephying the Laws of Physics

White Hawk Aviation Stories
My Brother's Keeper
Jungleland

Murder by Munchausen Series
Murder by Munchausen
The Darknet
The Invisible Mind

JUNGLELAND

WHITE HAWK AVIATION STORIES #2

BY

M.T. BASS

AN ELECTRON ALLEY PUBLICATION
MUDCAT FALLS, U.S.A.

Electron Alley Corporation
The Herald Building
732 Broadway Avenue
Lorain, OH 44052

This book is a work of fiction. Any references to historical events, real people, or real places are used fictitiously. Other names, characters, places and events are products of the author's imagination and any resemblance to actual events or places or persons living or dead is entirely coincidental.

Manufactured in the United States of America

Edited by Elizabeth N. Love (www.bee-edited.com)

Photography by Lora Mosier

ISBN 978-1-946266-16-3 (Trade Paperback)
ISBN 978-1-946266-15-6 (eBook)

www.MTBass.net

For LTC Harold H. Brown, USAF, Retired

Those that I fight I do not hate,
Those that I guard I do not love

~W.B. Yeats

Prologue

I forget who said the most exhilarating thing in the world is to be shot at without getting hit, but whoever it was, well, they got it wrong—at least for me. There are only two types of airplanes: fighters and targets. And if you're a fighter pilot you don't count the misses and paint them on the side of your crate. There's just no bragging about *not* getting shot after a mission. That being said, it had been fifteen years or so since I took enemy fire and it does have a funny way of focusing your attention.

~A. Gavin Byrd

*****~~~*****

Ella

Oh my God, it was hot. Always so damn hot. I couldn't wait to escape my cot under the mosquito netting in the morning to get off the ground, even though I knew it wouldn't be any cooler when I got back and landed. Relief—even temporary relief—was worth every second of it.

The jungle was simply gorgeous in the first light from altitude. Lush and green, mist frosted the treetops making Africa the mystical land I had read about in my youth and watched Johnny Weismueller swing through in all those *Tarzan* movies. In my adolescent daydreams, I was always the great safari hunter.

Now, I was a hunter of sorts—but for much bigger game than lions and elephants—leading a two-ship mission up a valley northwest of Kindu along the Lomami River in Congo. We were flying old T-6 Texans, out on an early morning search and destroy mission. Most of the guys I had flown with in England against the Germans, who stayed in the service, went on to make noise in jets over Korea. I'm sure that was *exhilarating*, but just not the same. This would be the closest I could ever get to climbing back into my P-51 Mustang again to sortie against Messerschmidts and Folke-Wulfs.

On my wing was Angel, one of the Cuban pilots who survived the Bay of Pigs fiasco and came to fight the Cold War again in Africa. We flew a loose formation, weaving up the valley, searching for Simba rebels our "intelligence" claimed were moving south. It was a messy business in the jungle, what with bandits and tribesmen moving in and out of alliances with the rebels and the Congolese Army depending on the greedy inclinations and the moods of their leaders that day. I didn't try to sort it out. I just flew in the direction they pointed and laid down ordnance on bad guys when we found them. There was no action so far this morning, and we lazily drifted up and down the valleys northwest of the base. If there were rebels or bandits in the area, we sure didn't want them paying a visit to our home away from home. They were known to be particularly ruthless and unforgiving. There's no Geneva Convention in "Jungleland."

Angel and I stayed off the radio, using hand signals to avoid announcing our position to eavesdropping ears below. We loitered in a loose formation, burning off fuel as slowly as possible to stay on-station—and up out of the heat—as long as possible.

Angel called "bingo" first, and we turned back towards the southeast for more gas in the tanks.

Sparks stood there waiting on the tarmac, hands on his hips, surrounded by the ground crew recruited from the locals, as I taxied in followed by Angel. Somehow, the mechanical magic man could tell just from watching us on final approach whether or not we had fired our guns or launched any rockets, so he started motioning the guys into position to refuel us once we were idling by the tank farm.

I swung the tail around and stood on the brakes. The crew started climbing all over the wings, dragging a pair of hoses to the fill ports. Angel did the same to my right, and his crew mobbed his plane as well.

Sparks climbed up next to the open canopy, a map in his hand being battered by the prop wash. He yelled in my ear, "It's a pisser, God damn it. New intel. Damn brainiac idiots."

I took the map and nodded. From the markings, our quarry was now evidently more to the north-northeast, so we'd patrol up that way next, heading north initially, then following the Lualaba River once we got to it.

Sparks slapped my shoulder and went to check that the fuel caps were secured. It would not have been the first time all the avgas got sucked out of the tank from ground crew carelessness. They meant well, but the Afrika Corps recruits he had to work with definitely weren't as good as regular Air Force crews, so Sparks kept a close eye on them.

I waited for Angel's crew to finish, then we taxied back out to the end of the runway. Maybe "runway," "airport," and "base" were too kind to the scar of land cleared out of the jungle for us to fly out of to help President Tshome and the CIA fight this hot ember of the Cold War here in sub-Sahara Africa. I didn't really care about the politics or economics. Only the flying. Though, it was pretty crude compared to what I enjoyed during wartime in Merry Olde England.

Without sliding the canopy shut, I advanced the power and started my take-off roll. Angel was at my four o'clock, and we climbed out, then turned north. The day was starting to heat up with the air getting bumpy, pushing us a little higher. We had a few months to go before the rainy season, so we flew nearly every day. When we got to the river, it was low and narrow in its banks, but still one of the best landmarks for pilotage. Angel and I turned northeast and began leaning out the mixture for best endurance.

Of course, it was no different here in Africa: hour after hour of nothing but the drone of your engine turning gasoline into noise, punctuated by mere minutes of the unmatched intensity of doing battle. Only, in this conflict, our focus was targets on the ground, not dogfighting—like at the end of the war, when the Luftwaffe had been decimated and what opposition they did throw up was quickly hosed out of the sky. At that point, we were like the Bears pummeling a hapless Northwestern Wildcats junior varsity team.

It was another three-quarters of an hour before anything happened. Sweeping southwest of the village of Nogabi, we started taking ground fire out of the jungle. The Simbas were amateurs with firearms. Their aim and firing discipline were so poor they were often more an annoyance than a threat, but over the winter months, they started to improve somewhat. The Simbas almost always forgot, though, that tracers work both ways, so once they opened up on us, they basically painted a bullseye on themselves.

"Break left," I radioed Angel, jammed the throttle forward, and yanked the stick back and to the left in a climbing turn to circle around on the enemy position. I searched back over my shoulder for a road or trail leading out of the area to anticipate their possible direction of movement. There was a small scar coming down off the hill to the southeast.

As we came around three hundred and sixty degrees, lining up on the small section of the jungle where red and green tracer rounds floated up our way, the intensity of the fire began to wane as the rebels understood what was about to come their way.

"Take the trail. Southeast," I radioed Angel.

He clicked his mike twice to acknowledge the one-two punch plan and throttled back to drift away in trail to follow up my initial attack on the enemy positions with rocket fire as they inevitably fled to melt back into the jungle.

I banked hard and began to dive down on the hilltop. The tracers began to concentrate on my nose. I lit up my guns, spreading the field of fire left and right with a little dance on the rudder pedals. I felt the Texan buck up a bit as rockets left the rails. I followed the plumes of their engines halfway to the target before I had to pull up, but noticed the intensity of the enemy fire had waned considerably.

"Way to go, Batman," Angel radioed. "Let me just clean up this little mess you made."

Behind me, Angel strafed the road and fired his rockets in so close that he seemed to clip the top of the fireball from the warhead explosions.

I circled back and took a path coming back up the road, stitching it with .303 caliber fire. Angel followed in my wake for one more pass, just to be sure. As we joined up to circle the position, I noticed some misting from Angel's right wing. He had taken a round in the fuel tank—an infamous golden BB—so I told him, and he beat feet back to the base before all the gas leaked out of his tanks.

I still had an hour or so of fuel and some unexpended ordnance, so I lallygagged my way home, exploring every nook and cranny of interest along the way. I half-heartedly kept an eye out for targets of opportunity, but mostly looped, rolled, and yo-yoed over the jungle, enjoying the relative coolness of altitude. There wasn't really much need to hurry back. I'd only have to loiter over the field waiting for the ground crews to deal with Angel's wounded bird and maybe clean up the runway if he leaked fuel or oil all over it.

I headed southwest and swung back around in a half-assed

patrol of the jungle surrounding the base down that way. There was little out there, aside from a couple of villages and a mission hacked out of the trees. I didn't see any activity and really didn't expect to. With the range on our planes, we were pretty safely tucked away from the rebel strongholds, though it never hurt to take a look-see to be sure the intel on enemy positions wasn't as bad as their other information. Me and Sparks would probably be the first to know if they were close enough to overrun us when Simba rebels sat down for dinner with us in the mess tent. Mainly, I just enjoyed the flying part—and its cool relief—while I could, until the reality of fuel burn brought me back to earth.

The base finally called all clear, so Angel must have made it back okay. I landed about forty-five minutes later. Taxiing back to the hardstand, I noticed a woman standing next to Sparks chewing his ear off and pointing at me. He dutifully absorbed the abuse, as if a long-suffering spouse, watching me shut down *White Hawk II* out of the side of his eye. He held her back with his arm as the prop blade spun down and finally stopped.

I slid back the canopy. The woman wriggled out from around the mechanic's blocking move and headed towards me.

Sparks shrugged his shoulders at my hand motion query. He folded his arms over his chest to watch the show.

The woman didn't even walk around the wing but stooped to cut underneath to take a more direct line towards me. She disappeared under the leading edge and appeared at the aileron, then followed the trailing edge back to the fuselage, looking for the handhold to get herself up on the wing.

I turned in the cockpit and watched her step up onto the wing and climb the incline up to me. I started to slide myself up to get out, getting my butt up on the back of the seat, but she got to me and blocked my way out.

"Just who do you think you are, mister?" she barked with the authoritative voice of a medical professional at the very top of the heap. I had heard that tone in my brother's voice more than a few times.

I just pulled off my helmet but left my mirrored Ray-Bans on. From safely behind the lenses, I carefully surveyed her gorgeously animated face—even in anger, her lips wrinkled in a bit of a smile as if this was half-show, half-genuine indignation. Her red hair was neatly pulled back in a ponytail, showing a freckled, fair complexion that had not yet been weathered and tanned by the sun, so she was new in country. Most of us outsiders knew each other well, but I didn't recognize who this was. I had heard about a new doctor at the mission, though never imagined it might have been female.

"You're not from around here, are you?" I asked.

"What?"

"I mean originally—not born and raised."

She scowled and punched my arm with her fist...*hard*.

"Ow!" I guessed she had at least one brother.

"Was that you—of course it was. Who else would it have been."

I unscrewed the plugs from my ears, and the volume level on her voice got louder. Over her shoulder, I saw Sparks shake his head and smile.

"Listen, mister—"

"Whoa, whoa, whoa there," I finally interrupted, holding up my hand, palm out like a cop stopping traffic.

She stopped talking and stared hard at me. She punched my arm again.

I cocked my head to the side. "Really?"

"Where in the hell do you get off shooting up my house calls?"

"Hi. I'm Hawk." I offered a handshake.

She slapped it away.

"All right. Doctor, I presume?"

"You're damn right."

"I'm still Hawk."

"As if I cared." She scowled at her reflection in my sunglasses. "You could take those off."

"I could."

"You might have killed someone."

"Well, I hate to tell you this, but that's kind of the point when you're getting shot at—you shoot back and not to tickle their toes."

"I wasn't shooting at you."

"I didn't say it was you. But tracer bullets don't naturally fall up from trees."

"But I —"

"You should be careful out there."

"I'm not part of that whole thing. I'm just here to take care of families."

"Yeah, well, rebels and bandits have families, too."

"Can you take those sunglasses off…Please?"

I did.

"Thank you."

"Try again? I'm Hawk."

She sighed mightily. "Doctor Mickleson."

"Why so formal? We're at least a thousand miles from the nearest *maitre 'd.*"

"*Doctor* Mickelson."

"Fine, then. If I ever need a prostate exam, I know who to call." I stood up on the seat to let myself out the other side of the fuselage.

She pouted when I turned away, then behind my back, I heard, "Ella. Ella Mickelson."

I turned around and held out my hand again. "I am pleased to meet you, Ella."

She eventually shook my hand but clearly didn't like it.

"And I am sorry about any misplaced ordnance that might have come your way. I had no intention of injuring any civilians…or you."

"Yeah…well…please be more careful next time."

"Can I buy you a cup of coffee?" It was still morning.

"No, thank you."

She spun on her heels, hopped down off the plane, and marched away towards a muddy and battered Range Rover.

"Glad to meet you, Ella," I called out. And I was.

But Dr. Mickleson ignored me and peeled out in her Range Rover, nearly spraying Sparks with clods of red clay.

"I guess she told you, doncha know," Sparks said when I came up beside him. He smiled an evil, knowing grin.

"You know, I think I feel a fever coming on." I put the back of my hand to my forehead.

"Maybe you should have that looked at."

"Hmmm. Maybe you're right." We watched Ella get swallowed up by the jungle. "Come on, I'll buy you a cup of coffee."

~~~

Alfalfa

The exhilaration of being shot at by Dr. Mickleson but not getting mortally wounded dissipated when I stepped into the mess tent with Sparks and saw Roscoe Pettis smiling back at me from one of the tables. He preferred to be called "Sarge"—but I called him "Alfalfa." One, because it visibly annoyed him; and, two, I refused to acknowledge any military rank whatsoever here in the jungle. Oh yeah, and three, he kind of reminded me of Spanky's partner-in-mayhem from *The Little Rascals*.

You would think that the local CIA man would make a bit more of an effort to appear to blend in, but he stuck out like a sore thumb with his neatly pressed white shirts, sharply creased khakis, and spit-shined jungle boots. Except for the boots, he looked like he just stepped off an Ivy League campus recruitment poster. His last posting probably could have been Yale or Harvard. He was a few years younger than me, and his baby face hid a hard-boiled personality tempered and sharpened by a tour of duty with the Marines in Korea, then working for "The Company" somewhere in southeast Asia before finding himself in Africa. He looked younger than he really was and more innocent than experience had left him.

"Look, Sparks, Alfalfa's here—What? Did Darla let you come out to play?" I pushed down an imaginary cowlick on the back of my head.

Sparks threw a scowl at the Company man, then went to grab a couple of cups of coffee. I pulled up a bench across from Roscoe, matching his grin, tooth for tooth.

"I heard you just met the new doc in town," Roscoe said with false enthusiasm. "What's she like, huh? I hear she's pretty."

I just smiled back, knowing he already knew everything about Ella and had probably met her, too, or what kind of spook would he be? Most likely a dead one, by now. But Roscoe was anything but incompetent.

"Gave you an earful, eh?"

"She seems to have at least a passing interest in aviation."

"Hey, Sparks. How's it going?" Roscoe greeted the mechanic as he sat down with a couple of cups of coffee.

Sparks just growled like a dog at a cat.

"Now, kids…" I said in the most paternal voice I could muster. "Don't make me turn this war around."

"Funny. Ha. Ha."

"So, what brings you out slumming the jungle?"

"I have to have a reason to visit my favorite merc?"

I rolled my eyes. I took a long, loud sip of bad coffee. "I keep telling you I'm not one of Mad Mike's boys. You guys hired me, remember? WIGMO?"

WIGMO was an acronym for Western International Ground Maintenance Organization. It was a CIA shell company that had a contract with the Congolese air force to provide "services." I unofficially slid over from flying cargo to spitting fire at the first chance I got. It was illegal for U.S. citizens to sign on as mercenaries. But nobody seemed to care. *Jungleland.*

"Whatever…had to get out of Dodge before the ambassador arrived." Roscoe sighed. "Too much pomp and circumstance for my taste. Besides, nothing exciting ever happened to me sitting at a desk."

"Can't argue with you there. Don't believe as I've ever actually had a real desk, so I don't know the stall recovery procedure for a Steelcase PT-19."

"Count your blessings."

I just nodded.

"Trust me, we don't have to worry about him showing up here, so I'm safe."

"And how goes the spy business these days?" Roscoe's day job was the worst kept secret in Africa.

"Well, you know, it's seasonal, and this is our slow time, so I'm taking inventory and cleaning up here and there—you know, trying to spruce the place up a bit to get ready for the holiday rush."

"Any big sales coming up?"

Roscoe pulled a folded up map out of his back pocket and slid it across the table to me, under Sparks' disdainful eye. The mechanic never did understand the currency of *quid pro quo* favors, but it helped to make sure that we had plenty of ammo and spare parts on hand, as well as steaks and beer in camp. Alfalfa's map would have some preferred flight plan deviation over some part of the jungle that Roscoe wanted checked out for his own reasons—I didn't really care what those were. Folded up inside would also be the cash he vouchered from some slush fund that I always passed on to the padre at the mission—it never hurt to be trading favors with one of the Lord's ambassadors, *quid pro quo*—just in case. Besides, I didn't need the money myself, and I kind of liked the idea of good coming out of Roscoe's special brand of evil.

"Careful over thataway." Roscoe tapped the map. "Injun country."

I nodded.

"Take a look-see in the T-6, then you and me will do a little bird-dogging." Roscoe stood up. "Oh, and don't get any ideas about Dr. Mickleson."

"Why, is she married or something?"

"Nah, but why would a good, young Christian physician want to have anything to do with a couple of reprobates like us?"

"Us? What do you mean 'us,' *Kimo Sahbee?*"

Roscoe just smiled his toothy Alfalfa smile.

"Don't even think about it, Roscoe. You'll blow your cover."

"Yeah. Right."

"The Company would not be pleased—not to mention Darla. It would be a black mark on your permanent record."

"That's why they call it 'black ops,' I suppose." Roscoe shrugged his shoulders and waved as he left the mess tent.

"Don't like that guy," muttered Sparks. He drained the last of the coffee in his cup. "Surely don't."

"You know, sometimes bad friends are better than no friends."

"Just don't like him. And damn sure don't trust him."

"He's CIA. Of course, you don't trust him. You never do. And never should."

Sparks just growled. *"Idiot."*

~~~**

Father Bob

Five hundred bucks of CIA money was folded up in the map that Roscoe slid my way. I skimmed five Jacksons off the top for walking around money and put the rest in the breast pocket of my flight suit for Father Bob. It was enough to feed the village for months. But before I ran it over to the mission, I figured I should check if we were done flying for the day.

I walked down to the operations shack to see who was around and what was going on. Eric was there at the duty desk, shuffling through papers. Ex-RAF, he was even neater and more fastidious about his attire than Roscoe.

"Hawk. Good show this AM," Eric said in his classic clipped accent. I had learned to speak British during the war.

"Our masters are pleased?"

"Oh, they will be as soon as I finish the damn paperwork." Eric shuffled paper left then right across the desk. "Patrol radioed, six confirmed."

"Any civilians hit?"

"No. But you may have rattled the cage of a nearby village, but they were but a thousand meters off or so."

A half-mile, I thought to myself. Close enough to get scared, but not hit—I wasn't so rusty as to miss by *that* much. You can't go around wasting ammo. "Good, then."

"Right-o."

"What's the report on Angel's bird?"

"Just a touch of salt and pepper. No real damage. Should be up tomorrow."

"So…today?"

"Stand down, lad. I've got Eduardo and Rafael set up for afternoon sorties."

"Okay, then. I'm going to head over to the mission."

"Careful, my good man." Eric cracked a wry smile. "There are reports of hostiles in that particular area."

Word traveled fast about my dogfight with Dr. Mickleson. I started to say something but just shrugged my shoulders.

From the operations shack, I wandered over to Maintenance. Sparks had his minions crawling all over Angel's plane.

"So, how's she look?" I asked, stepping up beside Sparks as he mumbled to himself.

"It's a pisser."

"How so?"

"If it was just the tank, we would have that patched pronto. But the damn round clipped a feed valve. Complicates things a bit."

"So, no go until…"

"He'll be grounded for a few days, till we get the part or I get it made myself. Gotta check with the boys downtown."

I nodded. Getting spare parts was only slightly more difficult than raising the dead. Looked like my plans for the evening might be coming together.

"Hey, Hawk," Sparks looked directly at me, "you ain't getting no ideas, now."

"Whatever do you mean?"

He shook his head. "It's a pisser."

Jungleland

I slapped him on the back and headed to my tent. I'd freshen up a bit—just in case the doctor was in.

~~~

After a shave and a quick bird bath, I got a reliable Jeep from Digby in the motor pool, loaded up and headed towards Father Bob's mission, northeast near the river. The Jeep was no sports car and the road was barely a road in spots—more like a dried out creek bed accidentally used as an avenue of sorts—so the going got slow at times and, even at that, still jarring to the spine. It was worth the trip, though, for some decent hot grub. Cooking was Father Bob's thing, and he somehow always managed to come up with a five-star meal out of one-star fixings.

"Like a Chinese restaurant: don't ask to see the kitchen, just enjoy the meal," Father Bob warned me at the beginning of our special relationship and, to be truthful, I don't think I actually tasted a morsel of that very first dinner, being that my mind churned with the ugly possibilities of what jungle creature I was consuming.

There aren't many motorized vehicles in the area, so the villagers are tuned in to the sounds of internal combustion engines, and there is just no sneaking up on them, especially in an old U.S. Army surplus Willys with a whiny transmission and a hole or two in the muffler. The greeting committee would be mostly kids if I got there in the afternoon or their fathers if it was closer to dinner time. I don't know where they went to work during the day, but it was just like back home that way: once the quitting time whistle blew, they were out on the streets—such as they were.

Even though I had to take it extra slow, since I had boxes of pharmaceuticals and medical supplies in the back, I got there around three, and kids swarmed around me like flies on a wildebeest. Chocolate didn't really work too well in the heat so close to the equator, but licorice did, so I passed sticks out from a bag until they had all run off with their prizes.

Ella watched from the door to her clinic, but I studiously ignored her, busying myself stacking up Father Bob's boxes of supplies in the back of the Jeep.

"Hawk, my boy," Father Bob called out as he came out of the mission building. "To what do we owe the honor?"

"Just a quick supply run."

He was a small, wiry man, who spoke and acted in quick, flitting bursts of energy. Before I even knew it, he was at my side, pawing through the boxes to see what I had brought. "Excellent. Excellent. I can't thank you enough."

I reached into my breast pocket and pulled out Roscoe's blood money. "And here. A little something to help the cause."

"I don't want to know, do I?" Father Bob asked with a knowing smile, snatching the cash from my hand as quick as a cobra strike.

"Yeah, kind of like a Chinese restaurant."

Father Bob winked and pocketed the envelope. We had an understanding about my tithes to his mission, and nothing more needed to be said about it. After all, I didn't need to bank the cash with my land holdings back in LA and my share of the air operations in Alaska—definitely not like the mission and the village did. Talk about a classic shoestring operation.

"Of course, you will stay for dinner, won't you?" Father Bob asked like a lawyer who already knew the answer to his question.

Jungleland

I nodded. "I thought you'd never ask."

"Oh, and you can meet our new physician, too." He chuckled and I swear that there was a damn sparkle in his eye when he said it. Jungle drums had no doubt informed him of our earlier dustup, and, evidently, I would be part of the floor show during dinner.

I looked back over my shoulder, but the doorway to the clinic was empty.

"I hear she's somewhat…spunky?"

"My boy, spunk is a wholly inadequate adjective."

"Hmmm."

"Maybe you'll see for yourself, come dinnertime."

"Maybe."

I grabbed my 7.62 FN rifle and hung it on my shoulder. Father Bob piled boxes against my chest until I could barely see over the top, then picked up the last two under his arms and scurried towards the clinic. I shuffled along slowly in his wake.

Inside the front door were a few moms and kids lining the walls of what passed for a "waiting room," though there was nary a *Life, TIME,* or *Reader's Digest* anywhere to be found to pass the time. Standing in the middle of the room, I was quickly surrounded by a gnatty cloud of kids again, their curiosity getting the better of their manners, while I waited for Father Bob to reappear from the back exam rooms. I don't know what the Swahili word for "licorice" is, but I was probably hearing it over and over again.

Father Bob came out, followed by Dr. Mickleson, costumed perfectly for her role in a white lab coat with a stethoscope draped over the back of her neck. He took only the top box and led me into the back to the storage room.

Ella's eyes and mine met as she tracked my passing as closely as a radar beam on an enemy bomber. I nodded, and she merely fell in line behind me.

"Thank you so much, Hawk," Father Bob gushed as he took the boxes one-by-one off my hands and put them on the shelves that were still less than half-filled after my supply run. I turned, and Ella's silhouette filled the doorway.

She suddenly began speaking to Father Bob in French. I didn't know what they were saying, but I swear I heard my name sprinkled in with their conversation as I followed them going back and forth.

Ella looked at me, then back at Father Bob.

Finally, he shrugged his shoulders and said, "Well, then, tell him."

"I wish you wouldn't bring those in here," she said, pointing to my sidearm and the rifle slung over my shoulder.

I followed her finger down to my holstered Colt 1911. "Honestly, I wish I didn't need to have them."

"This may not look like much, but it is still the village hospital."

"Oh, I know," I said, nodding but holding her glare. "But we're kind of close to a war zone. And a fella's got to be ready for anything—if he wants to make it back to his bunk at night."

Father Bob savored our little scene of character clash for a few humid moments—which, no doubt, enlivened the plotline of the little village soap opera he had going there—then stepped between us like a boxing referee with those final, unnecessary instructions before the bell rang. "I'm so sorry, have you been properly introduced? Ella, this is Gavin, Gavin Byrd. He's one of the pilots over at the base. They call him 'Hawk'—after your plane, isn't that right? Anyway, Hawk, this is our new country doctor, *Miss* Ella Mickleson."

Jungleland

Ella winced at Father Bob's blatant announcement of her marital status.

"How do, ma'am," I said catching Father Bob's twinkling eye and laying on the Midwestern farm boy charm as thick as I could. "Pleased to meet you."

"Mmm. We've met," Ella said warily to Father Bob.

"Right. Anyway. Dinner at six, my dear doctor? I'll be cooking something special for you and Hawk."

I smiled at Ella.

"I just can't wait."

"Excellent, then. Don't be late," Father Bob smiled wickedly as he led me out of the clinic and over to his "parsonage" near the chapel.

Along the way, he pumped me for news from the outside world, particularly regarding the see-saw battle between President Tshombe's Congolese Army "regulars"—aided and abetted by Mad Dog Mike Hoare and his merry band of mercenaries—and the Simba rebels in Stanleyville. I filled him in with what information I could—mainly that most of the action was still up north of the village and that the lines had been fairly static over the past few months. I assured him that the village and the mission should be largely unaffected, but that they should still be careful of infiltrators coming downriver. But, really, I wasn't telling Father Bob anything he didn't already know. His intel was far better than the government's and, most times, even Roscoe's. Sometimes I even half-thought that Alfalfa padded the blood money because he knew where most of it was going. *Quid pro quo.* Surely, he would call in that chit at the appropriate time.

"Oh, and thank you for *my* medicine," Father Bob said with a wink as he held up the bottle of scotch whiskey I had packed in with the pills and vaccines. He had deftly smuggled out it of the clinic right under the nose of Ella. "Care for an afternoon dose?"

I nodded, and he poured two glasses—neat, of course. No ice there in the village.

We sat, sipping in silence. I got the strange feeling Father Bob was sizing me up and calculating the odds on me for some kind of match up, no doubt with Ella. He may have been a man of the cloth, but he was a man, nonetheless.

"Think there's a chance?" I finally asked, reading his mind.

"Seven-to-one," he answered, rubbing his chin for a moment.

"Seven's a lucky number."

"Son, you're the underdog."

"Oh."

Father Bob gulped down the last of the scotch in his glass and hopped up to his feet. He poured another finger into my glass and headed towards the door. "I'm off to market for our dinner."

"What's on the menu."

"Ah, now son, you know the house rules."

I nodded.

"You sit here and relax a bit, and I'll commence to culinating as soon as I get back."

Before I could reply, he was out the door. I leaned back in the chair in his office, sipped my scotch, and vacuously scanned the titles on his bookshelf, until my head sank back. My eyelids involuntarily narrowed my view. The last thing I remember was a drop of sweat rolling down my temple before I dozed off.

~~~

Mmmm, garlic, I thought as I drifted back towards consciousness. I kept my eyes closed and drew in a deep breath of whatever Father Bob was preparing for dinner. I blindly took a sip of scotch and wondered how many suppliers besides me and the Red Cross he had to keep his missionary work—as well as his distinctly non-native lifestyle—going.

I became aware of a rustling beside me and rolled my head that way, slowly opening my eyes to bring Dr. Mickleson in the chair to my right into focus, sipping on a glass of whiskey and looking off and away from me, into the jungle beyond the window behind Father Bob's desk. I studied her profile.

"Good, then," I whispered to myself out loud, glad to see I wouldn't have to add a temperance battle over demon rum to our relationship.

"Pardon me?"

"Been here long?"

She held up her glass and visually measured the level of scotch, then said, clinically, "No. Not long."

I rolled my head back towards the ceiling, thinking that Father Bob was being overly kind in his odds-making.

Just then, he came in clapping his hands together and rubbing his palms. "Come. Come. Dinner is served."

Ella and I sat across from each other at the small square table out on what passed for a veranda, with Father Bob between us, ready and anxious for the show to begin. His housekeeper served us medallions of mystery meat covered with sauce and some kind of green vegetation. Ella looked at it suspiciously. I could tell she was tempted to ask but had probably gotten the same warning Father Bob gave me.

"So, Hawk's brother—" Father Bob interrupted himself and

looked at me.

Ella looked up and followed Father Bob's eyes towards me. "What?"

I shrugged my shoulders and nodded.

"So, Hawk's brother was a doctor, too."

"Was?"

"He met with some unfortunate—"

I interrupted Father Bob. "He was murdered. About ten years ago."

"I'm sorry." Her voice was sincere.

"Yeah. Me, too. He was a great guy, and I miss him."

"What did he practice?"

I took a deep breath, bracing for her reaction. "He was a plastic surgeon. In Beverly Hills."

Ella's jaw stopped in mid-chew, and she just stared across the table at me.

"Hollywood is its own kind of jungle. Believe me."

Ella slowly started chewing again. "So, what brings you here—I mean, besides your obvious love of humanity?"

"Actually, the weather."

"Seriously?"

"Hawk was living in Alaska," Father Bob jumped in. "You shouldn't be so quick to judge, my dear. He had his own bush pilot operation and was a veritable lifeline for so many of the native villagers there."

"I'll alert the Nobel Prize committee," Ella said with a sly smile.

"It was nothing really," I said with false modesty, playing along. "But I'd like to thank all those who made this award possible—"

"You haven't won anything yet, ace. Not here, anyway."

"Yes. Precisely," said Father Bob. "In fact, he was a fighter ace in World War Two. In England."

"A *real* ace?"

I shrugged my shoulders.

"Eleven? Is that right?" Father Bob asked.

"Eleven and a half."

"Can't forget that half," she teased.

"Hey. I earned it. The gun camera doesn't lie." I had to defend my record. "So, what brings you to Jungleland—I mean besides *your* love of humanity?"

"I just wanted to help—" Ella heard what she was saying and cut herself off. She smiled. "Truthfully? I did not want to spend my entire career in medicine—and my entire life, for that matter, as a hothouse orchid."

I nodded. "I understand."

"Really? What would you know about that?" she asked skeptically.

"Yeah, well, my brother wrestled with that in his own way," I said with weariness, remembering the circumstances of Stitch's death.

"Oh," was all she said. The tone of my voice must have told her that I really did understand.

"Ella studied at Georgetown and Harvard," Father Bob picked up the conversation. "We're so lucky to have her, thanks to her father's pull with the administration."

Ella winced visibly at the mention of her father.

"Must be nice to have 'pull' in the family," I said.

She smiled and carved into her medallions with a little more savage intent than surgical precision.

"Don't allow the sins of the father to visit upon..." Father

Bob trailed off. "He is what, my dear, a political adviser, or something?"

"A lobbyist. Started out as a lawyer, helping people, but now, he just pulls strings politically—you know, *pull*. It's evidently very lucrative."

I just nodded. Nothing to be gained in poking fingers into wounds still so obviously open and sore.

"Well, whatever. She is a godsend to us here," said Father Bob.

I smiled, looking across the table at Ella, staring into her beautiful brown eyes. I just nodded in agreement with Father Bob.

She caught the longing in my gaze. She smiled back softly, took a sip of wine, then averted her eyes coyly.

Father Bob sat back and watched. He knew.

Bird-dogging

I stayed a little longer than I probably should have and got back late to the base. It's not really safe traveling after dark through the jungle. You never know who or what you might run into—enemy soldiers, banditos, or other hungry predators. Plus, it was extra slow going at night in the Jeep on the "road." But dinner was tasty—whatever it was—and the company was, well, engaging and, truthfully, much more pleasant than what I expected—Ella, that is. No indignant speeches, just good conversation.

Father Bob is always a good time to be around, especially considering his profession. But then again, he came late to the cloth, having been an electrical engineer and successful businessman in his previous lifetime. Evidently, he held a few patents on some circuit designs used on diesel engines to monitor fuel efficiency. He made a fortune and traveled the world making locomotives, ocean-going freighters, and off-road construction equipment cost less to operate. Then he made an even bigger fortune when Cummins offered a deal to buy his company out that was just too sweet for him to refuse. About the same time, his wife decided half of everything without Bob would be better for her and her lover than everything together with him, so she kicked him to the curb. And it was there he found religion.

Father Bob was—and is—no fool, though. While he genuinely

wanted to do good, he didn't want to give up the good for himself, so he found a ministry that did not require a vow of poverty. In other words, he's no Jesuit. And, like me, he's got a tidy pile of money back home for himself—even after the legal vultures were done picking the carcass of his marriage clean. Why he picked Congo, nobody knows—though he says it's the one place he is sure not to run into his ex-wife. At any rate, breaking bread with Father Bob is always much more of an event than just shoveling chow into your pie hole. He's got a million stories of traipsing around the world to ride the rails or sail the seas in his quest for new orders. Of course, last night was a bonus of having that rarest of commodities there in the jungle, female company at the table.

I spent the ride home replaying dinner, savoring bits of Ella's conversation and the warmth of her smile that occasionally broke through the stern mask assumed by a medical professional, especially when she talked about things that brought her joy—riding horses, dancing, or early summer mornings at her parents' vacation home on the North Carolina outer banks, walking the beach alone to catch the sunrise and collect shells at low tide. I was still thinking about Ella when I got back to the base and found my way by moonlight to my tent. I started to strip down in the dark—no need to advertise for more bugs by lighting the lantern—to hit the sack.

"So, how's the padre doing?" Roscoe asked out of the dark.

"Jesus Christ!" I exclaimed breathlessly. "I nearly jumped out of my skin."

"Hey, I didn't ask about his boss," Roscoe said, sitting up on my cot. "Actually, forget those guys. How is Dr. Mickelson?"

"What the hell are you doing here?"

"I don't see any bleeding or bruising. Did you two kiss and make up?"

"Get out of my bunk."

"Sure. Sure. Just keeping it warm for you." Roscoe pulled a flask from his pocket and took a swig. He offered me a drink, but I shook him off like the hips of a dashboard hula dancer. He took a second swig. "Suit yourself."

"Again, to what do I owe the honor of your presence."

"Sparks said that Angel's plane will still be down tomorrow…today?" He squinted at the luminescent dial on his watch. "Yeah, today. So, I thought we could do a little bird-dogging. You know, the map I gave you."

I sighed heavily. "Can I at least get a couple hours of shuteye?"

"Oh, right. Sure. Sure." Roscoe hopped up from my cot. He passed close, pausing to whisper directly into my face. "So, you and Dr. Mickelson. Is that going to happen?"

I gave him the stink eye and pushed him aside, then stretched out on my cot.

"I'll just sleep here." Roscoe settled himself into a canvas deck chair and propped his feet up on my footlocker. He could sleep just about anywhere. "Sweet dreams, Hawk."

"Good night, Alfalfa," I said sternly. I threw my arm over my eyes, and before I knew it, I was thinking again of Ella as I drifted off.

~~

Roscoe woke me up before dawn with a cup of joe from the mess tent, which was almost as bad as LA police department coffee. Since we would be spending all day together in the little single-engine Cessna, he knew better than to agitate me first thing in the morning and put me in a bad mood.

Somehow Sparks knew and was there at the L-19 "Bird Dog" before Roscoe and me. "Morning, boys."

"Top of the morning to you, Sparks," Roscoe said way too cheerfully.

"You're all set, Hawk," Sparks said, ignoring the CIA man.

"Thanks." I nodded toward Roscoe and rolled my eyes back in my head for Sparks.

"It's a pisser." He nodded back at me.

I did a quick walk around, kicking the tires, checking the oil, and eyeballing the fuel level in the tanks. Sparks didn't take any offense. He knew the drill. It was my butt going up in the bucket, not his.

"After you, sir," I motioned for Roscoe to hop in the back seat of the tandem cockpit. I climbed in the front, adjusting my holster so it wasn't digging into my side. I put on my headset and pulled the bottom half of the door up. "Thanks, Sparks."

"Good hunting," he replied, handing me my FN FAL then stepping back beyond the wingtip. I set it alongside my seat.

Thoughts about Ella asking me not to bring weapons into the clinic the day before came to mind. I shook them off and went through the checklist to start the engine. The Lycoming jumped to life, bringing Eric to the door of the operations shack to watch us depart—off the books, of course. Everything Roscoe did was off the books. No paperwork—except for the greenbacks.

After a quick run-up, Roscoe and I were off, skimming the jungle canopy.

"Beautiful, huh?" he asked from the back seat.

"Shut up and let me just enjoy the view, at least."

Jungleland

Not a minute later, I heard Roscoe snoring over the intercom. I checked the map he had given me and banked to the northeast in the general direction of Lake Tanganyika. It was like the trees were evaporating up into the air with the morning mist. I wove back and forth to bust in and out of some low-level scud to give a sense of speed. Every once in a while, a flock of small colorful birds exploded from the jungle at our passing, like confetti blown out of a circus clown cannon. About ten minutes out from the red marks on Roscoe's map, I did a couple of steep banks and pulled some negatives Gs to wake him up.

"What'd I miss?" Roscoe asked.

"Not a thing."

"You would tell me, though. Right? I mean about the doc."

I shrugged, and he patted me on the shoulder. "Let's find the crossroads, head north twenty and fly a grid search out east and west for ten miles or so."

I nodded and picked up the east/west road and followed it into the sun until we got to a wider, paved road running north and south. I did a couple of tight three-sixties around the intersection. A pat on my shoulders confirmed this was the right spot, so I turned north towards the border and flew for fifteen minutes.

"I feel lucky," said Roscoe. "Let's start to the west."

I turned left, threw out some flaps, slowed to sixty-five knots, and started drawing imaginary squares in the air over the jungle. I could have asked what Roscoe was looking for, but I didn't really care, and even if I did—care or ask—he wouldn't have told me, so I just flew and enjoyed the peace and quiet while Roscoe did his thing behind me with his government-issued binoculars and Nikon camera.

The morning dragged on and on as we droned relentlessly over the jungle. I marked the time with grease pencil strokes on the side window for when I switched fuel tanks. It gave me something to do besides fly and try, unsuccessfully, not to think about Roscoe's mission, dinner last night…and Ella.

"We're going to have to find a watering hole," I said, making another grease pencil stroke on the window.

"To E'ville, then," Roscoe replied.

I turned south and followed the road to Elisabethville. Forty minutes later, we were taxiing up to a fuel tank by a large, nondescript hangar on the far side of the airfield. Roscoe bounded out of the plane and disappeared inside the hangar. I gassed up the tanks, then stretched my legs on the other side of the Cessna. I didn't know what went on inside the hangar and preferred not to know and not to meet any of the other spooks that might haunt the place. Knowing one was haunting enough.

Roscoe came back with some freshly made grinders and a couple of ice-cold bottles of Pepsi. We wandered off onto the grass to sit and eat our lunch. The government guys always eat good.

"They're getting better, aren't they?" Roscoe asked around a big bite of sandwich. I knew he wasn't talking about the cooks.

"I guess so. A little. Angel just got unlucky yesterday, but it always pays not to get too complacent."

"The Congo-line boys don't seem to have much fighting spirit." Roscoe chuckled at his pun.

"Yeah, well, that makes it easier for go-getters like me and Angel."

We gnawed on our sandwiches for a bit.

"I know what happened," Alfalfa said.

"What do you mean?"

"In Alaska. The State Department weasels threw you under the bus, right?"

I nodded.

"I checked up on you, you know." Roscoe stared me down.

"Yeah, well, I got the job done, anyway."

"Eh, they're all rat bastards in Foggy Bottom. So, what do you expect?" Roscoe smiled. "And now you're here."

"Yeah, kind of a change of scenery, I guess."

"Well, we take care of our own."

"Good…*I guess.*"

"You didn't expect to make this a long term career, did you?"

"Something I should know about?" I asked.

"It's just time catching up with history. The colonial days are dying. The Brits in India. The French at Dien Bien Phu. The Germans, Dutch, and Belgians here in Africa."

"I didn't know you were such a history scholar."

"Pays to know the lay of the land—especially the lay of the land where you lie."

I ignored his high hanging curveball about honesty. "So, are you saying this is an unplayable lie?"

"It ain't tilting at windmills. It's fire and ice, my friend. Hot embers in a cold war."

"Meaning?"

"You're not doing this for the coin, right? I mean, the mercenary thing."

"Really, I don't think any of us are."

"Right. You and Father Bob, though, huh?"

"He's got his reasons. I've got mine."

"Sparks?"

"He's got nothing to worry about. He'll be taken care of."

Roscoe looked me in the eye. "And Dr. Mickelson?"

I just took a bite of my sandwich. "We all have our demons. Hers might be her father."

"Yeah, well, so be it. Everybody's got to have an out, though."

I looked at Roscoe, but he refused to meet my eye. He was obviously skating close to the edge.

"You got an out, Hawk?"

I shrugged my shoulders.

"Might be time to give it some thought. When things get ugly, the ugly splatters everywhere. When it does, well, that's not really the best of times to be counting seats in the lifeboat."

We sat in silence on the grass, eating our sandwiches and drinking good old American Pepsi-Cola.

When we finished, I asked, "So, we heading back North?"

"Nah. I saw what I needed to."

"Okay, then. Home it is."

"It's good to have friends and all, but it's better to have a plan."

"Plan your flight and fly your plan?"

"Yeah. Something like that," Roscoe said flatly.

I don't know what Roscoe saw in the jungle, but it didn't seem to have put him in a good mood.

~~~

Eric the Red

When we got back to the base, Roscoe thanked me with another envelope for Father Bob—this one was extra fat, which confirmed the flight's importance—and headed back to wherever he comes from. No one really knew where Roscoe lived or went to work every day. I wandered over to the operations hut where Eric was sitting at his desk shuffling through paperwork.

Eric was a pasty-faced Brit with reddish-blondish hair that probably betrayed some ancestral straying across the northern border with Scotland sometime in the past. Who knows, we might have even been kin. He was less fastidious with his dress than his paperwork. I never saw him outside the base and couldn't recall him actually taking leave to go to the capital city for any R&R.

"What's the good word, Red?"

"Angel will be flat-footed for another day. Sparks is waiting on a part—unless you want to run to E'ville to get it."

"Sure. Why not. I've got nothing planned."

"Good, then. You can take the twin Beech. I'll have it gassed up, and you can leave directly."

"Is the part that big?"

"No, but I've got some other supplies you can retrieve," Eric said with a wry smile. He was like a master puppeteer, pulling strings up and down the supply chain to get better food, drink, and recreation for us—and himself. Eric's "habit" was one he acquired in India. No one spoke of it and it did not get in the way of his duties—here anyway. The Royal Air Force had other opinions, which is why he found himself in Congo, with the rest of us retread warriors. He handed me a fist full of paperwork and an envelope, then took a sip of tea, winking at me over the brim of the cup. "This should cover it with the gang down there."

I nodded and took the papers. I got used to hanging back on the fringes. Too much information was, well, too much sometimes.

"You might want to pack an overnight bag. Not sure if you'll make it back before dark."

I waved the paperwork and went back to my tent to throw a change of clothes and a shaving kit in a bag. I didn't hear the Range Rover pull into camp and didn't notice it parked outside the operations shack when I cut across the hardstands to the Beech 18. The plane was exactly similar to Seven-Sugar-Papa, which I had flown up and down the coast of California too many times to count and had left behind in Alaska. I liked flying that plane. This one, too.

"Get me that part and I'll have Angel flying in a couple of hours," Sparks said, greeting me at the cabin door. He had it opened, thankfully, to let a little of the midday heat out of the fuselage.

"No problem." I tossed my bag inside, climbed in, and made my way to the cockpit.

"Oh, ah, Hawk," Eric called out to me, sticking his head in the cabin door. "You wouldn't mind adding a mission of mercy to your itinerary, would you?"

"How's that?"

"Something of a dreadful accident and all."

"How long before we can leave?" It was Ella's voice behind

Eric and outside the plane.

"No problem," I answered Eric and headed back their way. When I got to the cabin door, she was grilling Eric on the details of when we would depart and how long it would take to get her patient to Elisabethville.

"If he doesn't get to a hospital soon, he might lose his leg—or worse."

I said nothing as I slipped by to pre-flight the plane, but her eyes followed me as I worked back around the empennage to check the elevator and rudder. "Can't we hurry up?"

"It shan't be too long a flight, and Hawk, here, should be ready to go straight away. Safety first, you know. Now, let's get your patient on board while he makes the final preparations. I shall alert the medical folks there to expect your arrival."

Ella supervised the moving of her patient, a village man I guessed, out of the back of the Range Rover and into the plane. I came back around the left wing and stood back as they loaded him in. She looked at me like she wanted to say something about the urgency of the situation but didn't. She got into the plane and tended to the positioning of the man on a stretcher in the cargo hold by two large village men. When they were done, the one—a giant of a man—gave me a menacing look, then backed away from the plane, watching me closely, suspiciously.

Once Ella and her patient were settled, I climbed in and pulled the cabin door shut. The man's leg was bandaged, but he was bleeding through the gauze. They covered the man carefully with a blanket that he shivered beneath. He didn't look good, so I dispensed with any pleasantries and expedited the rest of the checklist to depart as quickly as we could.

The flight to E'ville was uneventful for me, but it was probably the first time the villager had been at any altitude to speak of, though he didn't seem to be too conscious of his surroundings, being distracted as he was by the pain.

I contacted the tower with a "Lifeguard" call sign and explained the situation, which got me to the front of the line for landing. As I taxied up to the ramp, an ambulance parked beside us before I had even shut the engines down. I looked back over my shoulder and watched them take the wounded villager out of the plane. Ella followed him out. She looked back at me in the cockpit one last time, then, without a word, deplaned and got in the back of the ambulance.

Once the ambulance was on its way to the hospital, I got up out of my seat and walked back to the cabin door. A pool of red was left on the floor where the stretcher had been. Butterflies gathered to lap up the blood like wildebeests and roan at a veld watering hole. I went into the hangar to find some rags and a bucket to clean it up, wondering if the villager would make it. Between waiting for the plane to be loaded and for Ella to be done at the hospital, I had some dead hours on my hands, so I went across the street from the airport to Ernie's Midway.

Ernie's was a bar run by an ex-pat from Chicago. Its charm consisted of cold, cold beer and hot, fresh, and greasy hamburgers that reminded me of home. Ernie was a die-hard Cubs fan, while me and my brother followed the Sox, so there was always plenty for me and Ernie to debate as I slaked my thirst and waited for my good, old American cheeseburger to emerge from the kitchen.

"They said you were here," Ella's voice came from over my shoulder.

I turned on the barstool to face her. "How's the patient?"

"He didn't make it. Lost too much blood."

"Sorry."

"Well, at least you gave him a chance. Thank you."

I shrugged and motioned to the stool beside me. "I'll buy you a beer and a burger."

Ella nodded her head and sat down beside me. I could tell by the sudden slump in her shoulders and the cant in her head when her neck muscles relaxed that the adrenalin rush of the medical emergency had collapsed. Combat was the same way. You supercharged your body with its own drugs, and you were pushing the sound barrier. But once the danger passed, you came back to earth. Sometimes hard. I motioned Ernie to put in a kitchen order for Ella and bring two more beers. She closed her eyes and rubbed the bridge of her nose.

I gently patted, then rubbed the top of her shoulder. She didn't resist or pull away. There was nothing to say, really. Stitch taught me that, so I didn't.

Ernie brought us two long-neck Simbas. "You need a glass, ma'am?"

Ella shook her head. We clinked our bottles in a silent toast and drank. Ernie brought out my cheeseburger. I signaled him with my head, and he served it to Ella.

"That was quick."

"Can't beat Ernie's for service."

She flipped the top and checked out the burger. "Looks good. Is it…?"

"We ain't in the jungle. And Ernie's not Father Bob." I smiled. "Dig in. Don't wait for me."

"God, thanks." She topped off the burger with mustard and ketchup, then dug in with gusto. "I didn't realize how hungry I was."

I smiled. At least there was one thing in common: the love of a good burger. It was a start.

I let her enjoy her meal in peace. Halfway through her burger, I got mine. Just then, one of the ramp rats from across the street came in to tell me that the plane was loaded up and ready to go. If we left right then, we could just get back to the base before dark. I slipped him a couple of bucks, whispered that we'd head back in the morning, and asked him to arrange for a couple of rooms for the night. Then, I souped up my burger—thinking better of the onions, this time—and joined Ella.

We ate in quiet. When we had both pushed our plates away, Ernie came to trade them for a couple more longnecks. Ella took a long pull, then rested her elbow on the bar and her head in her palm and looked me over.

"I know why I'm here. And I know why Father Bob is here. But what about you, Mr. Fighter Pilot?"

I smiled. "Ah, you know, we're not really dogfighting out there. Air-to-mud missions."

"Yeah, but why fight at all?"

No real good answer to that one, so I just shrugged.

"I mean, I'm here to save bodies. And Bob is here to save souls…" She said it without the malice I had expected after our first encounter on the wing of my plane. "From what Bob tells me, you don't need the money."

"That is true." I nodded and took a swig of my Simba. "But that's just a happy coincidence. I guess I'm lucky that way, but it's never been about the money—and never had to be."

"What then?"

I tried and failed to keep a slight grimace off my mug.

"Are you of Belgian descent?"

"Nah. Scottish. I might even be Eric's seventeenth cousin removed—as far removed as possible, I hope."

"So, how did you end up here?"

It was a good question, the answer to which I had never really articulated. "You mean, here at Ernie's with a pretty, young doctor?"

"Here in the jungle. In the middle of a civil war."

"It's closer to the equator than the Arctic Circle."

"Ah, so you came for the weather."

I smiled. "There's heat…then there's heat."

She nodded as if she understood, then took a long drink of her beer. Ella looked me straight in the eye. "I'm not buying the weather thing. You here to help Roscoe fight the Commies?"

"You know about Roscoe?"

"It seems everybody does."

I shook my head. "It's why the Cubans are here. They hold a hell of a grudge against Castro. But not me. Never knew the guy."

"Not the money…not the politics…probably not religion…so, then, what's left?"

"…a lonely impulse of delight…perhaps."

"What's that mean?"

"I didn't hate the Germans—except for that wallpaper hanging son-of-a-bitch. Everybody hated him. But the flying…"

"Oh, I get it, *Knights of the Sky?* Always struck me as a cold and impersonal way of fighting a war."

"Most people think that."

"And?"

"Most people have no idea. It's rat-wrestling, eyeball-to-eyeball, bending the hell out of your airplane, 'cause at the end of the day, you're either gonna be a tiger or a movie star."

"Movie star?"

"Caught on film…in the victor's gun camera. Cold? Yeah. It's bloodsport. Impersonal?" I shook my head. "Nobody else gets pictures of their bullets and cannon shells hitting home."

"And you are a tiger?"

"Eleven times. Then the war ended."

"Don't forget the half."

"There's nothing like it. No excuses. No slack. All on the line."

Ella shook her head. "And who cleans up after?"

I shrugged my shoulders. "You do, I guess. And Father Bob."

"The man you tried to save today. He was just a tribesman. And maybe he helped the rebels. I'm not sure he really had much choice. But his accident was getting too close to shrapnel. Maybe even some of yours."

I met Ella's questioning gaze.

"Did you capture that on film?"

I sighed. "You do know what they do—the Simba rebels. How they treat their victims. Right?"

Ella flinched. "I've heard…"

"You've heard right. Brutal. Indecently inhuman. Who cleans up that mess?"

After a moment, we both took a pull off our beers, eyeballing one another down the length of our bottles.

"We're not so different, you and I, as we practice our respective crafts," I said.

"How do you figure?"

"Would you have done anything different if he had been a rebel?"

Ella thought for a moment, then shook her head.

"Or an…*incorrigible* like me?"

She smiled.

"Me, too, neither—huh." I finished my beer and signaled Ernie for another round.

"Great. Another complicated man to deal with—and way out here in the middle of the jungle, no less."

"Is complicated good?"

"Sometimes. Sometimes not. The jury's still out on you."

I shrugged my shoulders and started in on my next beer. I could feel Ella watching me, studying me.

"Just remember," she said, picking up her fresh long neck, "whatever you say can and will be used against you."

"In a court of law?"

"Something like that. After all, my father is an attorney. Maybe worse."

We finished our beers and found our way to the hotel where the Fixed Based Operator had set us up with two rooms, which were across the hall from one another.

"Good night, Doc."

"'Night, Hawk." Ella smiled and slipped into her room, closing the door quickly behind her.

I paused, then went to bed myself.

~~~

Tracers

I was up early and headed back to Ernie's for some of his famous scrambled eggs and pepperoni, a delicacy I never failed to enjoy if I overnighted in E'ville. When you see your name in the paper too many times, like I had during the whole ugly mess with Stitch's murder in LA, you start to avoid reading the daily rags—unless, of course, you live for that sort of thing—like the Hollywood crowd. So, I caught up on current events from my favorite bartender and anchorman, Ernie. He filled me in on the latest in politics and sports from back home, though I discounted his assessment of the White Sox's chances for the season. After all, he's a Cubs fan, and what would he know, really, about winning?

I lingered over a second cup of coffee, hoping that Ella would get my note at the front desk and join me, but apparently a real bed, instead of a canvas cot, held its own charms. I paid Ernie and headed across the street to the airport. I tended to the paperwork for Eric's cargo, then went to inspect that it was properly loaded for weight and balance. I checked the manifest, did some quick mental calculations, and ordered up fuel.

As I watched the refueling, a man wandered up. He stood off a bit, looking around the tarmac. With his hands shoved into his pants pocket and a satchel draped over his shoulder, he watched them pumping gas into the tanks.

When the line boys finished and left, the man took a step

towards me and asked with a French accent, "Do you have my envelope?"

"What?"

"The envelope? From Eric?"

I turned and looked back at the offices to see if anyone was watching.

He stepped over close. He opened the satchel and showed me a wax paper package of white powder. "The envelope, please."

I went into the plane and got the envelope. He met me at the door.

He grabbed the money and quickly pressed the package into my hand. *"Merci beaucoup."*

I sighed as he spun around and wandered casually off the tarmac. I put Eric's drugs into my flight bag.

There was nothing more to do but wait for Ella, so I wandered out to the edge of the ramp to watch the morning's activities at the airport. Planes came and went at a regular but leisurely pace. It wasn't LAX. It wasn't Alaska either, where my arrival in some native village was like the big social event of the week. Of course, it was in a way. I brought essential supplies and sometimes special visitors or returning tribal dignitaries. I took away the sick and, sadly, occasionally brought home their bodies.

It made me feel like one of those barnstormers from the era between the wars, when aviation was still new and exciting for everybody—pilots, passengers and ground-pounding gawkers alike. Alaska was a place where you could still see the awe and admiration in the eyes of adults as well as the kids. And after a while, I got to know folks and families I was serving in a way that an airliner captain never could—at least the ones behind the regulars in first class. They were always glad to see me land and a bit sad when I took off. It was a hard life for men and machines, but one we all shared together. I think I would have gone on there for a long time if it hadn't been for that mess with the State Department. The country was beautiful and I really didn't mind the cold as much as what I told people. My blood thickened up. Just an excuse, really.

As I watched a Sabena Airlines plane on final approach, Ella suddenly appeared at my side.

"Good morning," she said.

"Sleep well?"

"A real bed? What do you think?"

We watched the plane touch down and taxi in.

"That's the kind of plane I came here on," Ella said, raising her voice to be heard after we watched the airliner lumber by on the way to the terminal building.

I watched her shake her head in an innocently seductive way as the prop wash mussed her hair, pushing it across her face. "A Douglas DC-4."

"Have you flown those?"

"Nah." I shook my head. "I'm not one for crowds on the ground, let alone aloft."

Ella looked at me and pulled a strand of hair out of her mouth.

"Did you get any breakfast?"

She shook her head. "I think I better not. I can eat when we get back."

"You sure? Ernie has real eggs, not powdered."

"Yeah. I think I just want to get back."

"Suit yourself."

We walked back to the Twin Beech, and I did a quick walk

around again to check the fuel caps and pull the chocks. Ella waited at the cabin door. I motioned her to step up, followed her in, and pulled the door closed. She stood in the middle of the cabin as if looking for her seat assignment.

"Come on up front." I pointed her towards the cockpit.

"Really?"

"Be kind of lonely back here. No Sabena stews aboard."

We walked up the incline to the front of the plane, and I pointed to the right seat. Ella got in and looked around, clearly out of her element surrounded by the gages, switches, and knobs on the panel and pedestal. She leaned forward to look out over the nose.

"How can you see out?"

"We'll waddle our way to the runway, and once we're airborne, it'll be easier. You'll see."

She gave me a curious look. I pulled out the checklist and started going through it out loud, a little more slowly and deliberately than usual so she could more easily follow along—a bit of a show, but sometimes it helps put the uninitiated a little more at ease by letting them in a bit and taking the complete mystery out of the process. I watched her follow my hands intently as they moved around the cockpit.

"Ready?"

Ella nodded.

I slid my side window open and hollered, "CLEAR!"

I swept the perimeter around the left wing then cranked the engine. The radial coughed and belched then caught. The racket swept a look of concern across Ella's face. I looked over at the right engine, and when it began to crank, she looked out her side window. I fiddled with the throttles to get them idling smoothly and watched the oil pressure holding steady. Ella looked over and smiled hesitantly. I smiled back, unlocked the tail wheel, and released the parking brake. I put on my headset and pointed to hers. She took them off the hook. She tucked her hair behind her ears and slipped them over her head.

Ground control quickly had us S-turning our way out to the runway. Ella watched everything going on inside and outside of the cockpit like a wary cat. After the run-up, we had to hold short for a C-124 Globemaster on final approach. Out of habit, I did a final check by rote—controls free, instruments set, fuel on mains, flaps set, trim set for take-off, radios set—then settled in to wait for the four-engine cargo plane to cross the fence and land. Ella stared out towards the speck in the sky that was the Globemaster. I soaked in her delicate profile. I smiled a little when I realized that she had gone to the trouble of putting on make up for the flight from civilization back into the jungle in this old bucket-of-bolts cargo plane. In the harshly practical and metallically industrial business end of an airplane, her beauty was like a flower sprouting in a sidewalk crack.

The unmarked C-124 approached quickly from the right and suddenly filled the cockpit windows, its engines rattling the fuselage of the Beech 18 and trailing smudges of black from their exhaust stacks. Ella's head panned quickly to follow it touch down with blue-gray puffs of smoke blossoming from the mains. She looked at me and smiled with wonder in her eyes.

I flipped on the fuel pumps and the inverters. A moment later, the tower called and instructed us to taxi into position and hold. Ella leaned forward to watch the cargo plane clear the runway. I locked the tail wheel. The tower cleared us for take-off, and Ella glanced over at me, a somewhat helpless look on her face, like maybe she didn't know what she was getting herself into. Yeah, me too.

"Ready?" I asked.

Ella smiled, then nodded.

I smiled back and pushed the throttles forward. Soon the tail was up and we were flying.

After we turned on course, I stayed low over the savannah—five hundred feet or so. The plane bucked a little, but it was still early, so the thermals weren't so bad yet. I really didn't want the time with Ella to pass quickly, but I needed to see and feel speed, as if the low-level visual blur could also blur the past.

I watched Ella closely and, though her grip on the armrest was tight, she looked like someone enjoying a roller coaster ride, not frozen in terror. So we flew north towards the scar in the jungle I called home…for now.

Suddenly, a wave of *deja vu* swept over and saddened me, sitting again in a Beech 18 with a gorgeous woman beside me—just like I had done so many times with Elaine back in Seven-Sugar-Papa, flying up and down the California coast.

I only got together with Elaine a few times on the occasional trips back to LA, but I had seen every one of the movies she edited and directed—once they finally made their way up to theaters in Alaska. I could have stayed with her at Stitch's house when I visited. There was certainly enough room, but it never felt right, so I didn't. The last time I came to town to finalize everything with Al McGuire before I came to Africa, I didn't even call her. Now, with Ella sitting to my right instead of Elaine, I wished I had, and my smile waned.

"What are you thinking about?" Ella asked.

"Huh?"

"I know that look."

"Nothing."

She shot me a squinty-eyed gaze, then leaned over and punched me in the right arm—hard, but not so bad, really.

"Ow!"

She smiled back at me. "I'll get it out of you before we land."

"It's a long story."

"We've got time, right?"

I twisted in my seat like I was cutting a couple of buttonholes with my back side. "It's nothing."

She squinted and raised her arm again.

"Okay, okay. When I lived in Los Angeles, I used to fly for a guy named Al McGuire out of Van Nuys. And he had a Twin Beech like this one, and I used to pick up flights running checks up and down the coast."

"Checks?"

"Yeah, banks trying to move their money around as quick as they can. Anyway, I had a friend in the movie business that I used to take along every once in a while."

"A friend?"

"She used to be an actress, but..."

"Oh, I see, now."

I looked out my side window at the passing grassland. "She had a bad car accident that really messed up her face. I told you my brother was a plastic surgeon, right? Well, it took a while, but he fixed her up. You know, for free."

"You liked her, though, right?"

"Yeah, but, really, she was more interested in Stitch."

"Ouch."

I shrugged.

"And then your brother was killed?"

"That was another whole big mess." I fiddled mindlessly with the prop levers pulling them out of sync and putting them back in again.

"And then you went to Alaska?"

I nodded.

"Is she still in the movies?"

"Not on the screen anymore. You know how that works." I shook my head. "Mainly as a film editor. She's directed a couple of films: *Fear of Falling* and *Lost Angels*.

"I saw *Fear of Falling*. It was good."

"It's a tough business."

"Yeah, I get it."

I nodded. "Which is why you are here, right?"

"I didn't want to be just a private practice pediatrician, you know?"

I chuckled. "Yeah, and now you're taking care of all those kids."

"And gunshot victims." She looked out across the plains. "I guess I get some credit for being in a war zone."

"You going to be here long?"

"I promised my dad I'd be back in a year…maybe."

"He didn't want you to come, right?" I looked over.

She sighed. "You know fathers and their little girls. I suppose he just wanted me to get married and get a house in suburbia and have kids and all."

"But?"

"Well, I just don't do well stuck indoors."

I smiled. "So, he doesn't always get what he wants."

She grinned back. "Not this time."

Jungleland

Out my window, I saw a herd of antelope. I pointed them out to Ella. "Hang on."

I arced the Twin Beech left and let it slide down until we buzzed them at a hundred feet, chasing them off through the plains.

I smiled at Ella, then climbed back up to altitude.

"That was fun," she said.

"You have no idea." I smiled.

We droned on and on lost in our thoughts. The browns of the savannah gave way to the green of the jungle until, without warning, tracers began to sprout up and reach out to us from the jungle. Ella smiled in fascination at the slow, blossoming fireworks, then furrowed her brow as the tracers streaked by the windscreen in the instant before I instinctively began to jink the plane off its straight and level flight path, first right, then left. I pushed the prop levers and throttles forward to full power and high RPMs and pulled into a sharp climbing turn back to the right. Gravity pulled back on my guts towards our original flight path. I could feel the impact of rounds on the rear of the fuselage. I rolled back left, bunted the nose over to gain speed, catching a moment of negative Gs and praying that they didn't hit the fuel tanks. I cranked us over and up to the right again.

I couldn't shoot back.

As quickly as the attack had come upon us, it was over and we were cruising along at five thousand feet, the feeling of speed replaced by a sense of awakening from the haze of a dream.

"You okay?" I asked Ella. Her face was pale.

She nodded, clearly frightened now.

I smiled and shrugged my shoulders, but wondered whether those were rebel or bandit rounds coming our way so close to home. Then I recognized that we were near the area that Roscoe had me fly the search grid for him. I didn't like where my thoughts were leading.

I noticed a bullet hole in the sidewall of the cockpit and checked Ella over carefully to make sure that she was okay and not literally in shock from a wound. She was breathing heavily, but not bleeding.

"No golden B-Bs today," I said, taking her hand and squeezing it to assure her everything was all right.

"What do you mean?"

"Small arms fire is usually more bark than bite—unless that one magic bullet improbably finds its way to just the right spot to clip a fuel or hydraulic line and cause a real problem."

She looked at me skeptically. The first time under fire is always the worst.

"We should be… *exhilarated* that they missed, I guess."

I glanced at the bullet hole again but didn't point it out to her. We flew on in silence, and before long, I started our descent to land—a little too soon for my tastes as that meant unfriendlies were definitely too close to home for comfort.

I landed and taxied to the hardstand. Almost before the props had stopped spinning, Sparks was inside the plane rummaging through the cargo for the part he needed to get Angel's plane flying again.

"Hawk! Get your ass—" he started to call out, then saw Ella peering back from the cockpit. "Oh…Eric is looking for you."

I just nodded. I definitely didn't want to say anything about his drugs. I grabbed my flight bag. "I better go see what he wants."

When I got outside the plane, Father Bob was there waiting, surrounded by armed tribesmen. Beside him stood the tall, black man who saw us off the day before. He stood smiling broadly with his arms resting on the pistols in his belt.

"Here to bring Ella back to the village," Father Bob said more seriously than I'd ever heard him speak—even at a funeral service.

The tribesmen looked around curiously. They carried AK-47s over their shoulders.

"No need to worry. Just a bit of insurance."

But I didn't believe him. I looked back at Sparks helping Ella step down out of the plane.

"Simon?" she asked.

"Good morning, Dr. Mickleson," the man beside Father Bob said in a low, clear voice with a heavy French accent.

"I'm sorry," Ella said sadly. "We tried very hard. But they couldn't save him."

Simon's smile slid off his face. "I understand. Come now. Let us go."

Ella looked back at me, then quietly followed Simon to the Range Rover.

Father Bob just shook his head and went after them.

I watched them leave, getting swallowed up by the jungle. When they were gone, I headed for the operations shack.

~~~

The Ferret

I noticed the Ferret armored car parked outside Eric's operations shack along side a couple of beat-to-hell Jeeps.

"What the…?" I started to ask Sparks.

"Yeah. Pleasant fellows—*idiots*. Made themselves right at home, drinking our coffee and eating our grub."

"Hoare's guys?"

"Five Commando. Here for our protection, *evidently.*"

"Against what?"

"We probably don't want to know. Leastways, I don't."

"I wonder what Alfalfa has to say about it."

"Ain't been around. Don't think he cares much for the fellows neither." Sparks stopped to kick at red clods of clay. "You think it's a good idea to keep hanging out around these here parts with this band of colorful characters we got going on? It's a freakin' Looney Tunes cartoon what with the fancy-pants Pepe le Pew Frenchie types, the Speedy Gonzales boys, and now these South African pit bulls Mad Mike calls soldiers. Not to mention the Man with the Golden Arm. Or Mr. Cloak-and-Duggar, himself."

I looked down the empty road that took Ella and Father Bob away, back to the mission.

"Don't know what yer thinking there, Hawk. But it's a damn sure bet it ain't safe for them. Especially her."

I thought about what Roscoe said about having an out.

"Eric wants me to fix Angel's bird. Pronto."

"Must mean he wants us back in the air," I said.

"I suspect so." Sparks sighed. "Anyways, I'll see to it."

Sparks headed off to the hardstand where Angel's plane was parked. He stopped to look back at me, then continued on.

I went into the operations shack. Mercenary types were scattered haphazardly in chairs around the briefing room. They were marginally uniformed and heavily armed.

Eric nodded my way, then turned his attention back to the three men sitting at his desk. One was a neatly coiffed and dressed Belgian officer; the other hadn't been near a barber's chair in a couple of months. He also obviously didn't have the benefits of local dry cleaning that the Belgian enjoyed. The third man was a Congolese Army officer—also nattily dressed—who sat impassively with his arms folded across his chest and a bored look on his face.

I hung back and surveyed the mercenaries. One slept sprawled across a bench in the back of the room. Another's head bobbed as he repeatedly dozed off and woke himself when his chin hit his chest. Three stood at the window, looking out and carrying on a conversation, the gist of it being a running complaint about being stuck in some backwater away from the action. The last commando, with stripes on this sleeve, sat digging something out of the palm of his hand with a dagger.

A lot of people poo-pooed them for their lack of military discipline and spit-shine, but they were plenty tough enough for the street brawl being fought there in the jungle—and plenty ruthless themselves to deal with the ruthless Simbas.

I went over and sat down next to the Sergeant poking himself with the blade.

Jungleland

He looked over at me. He pointed at my 1911 with his dagger and asked with a South African accent, "Is that for show or you got ammo for that thing?"

"I got what I need."

"Good for you. You can never leave too big a hole."

I nodded. Nine-millimeter ammunition was easier to get, but like the South African said, stopping power is everything. "You boys just passing through? Or…"

He shrugged. "I go where they tell me. Get paid one way or another. Just like you. Don't really care 'cause it ain't my country."

"True enough."

"Those three, on the other, hand…" The sergeant pointed to the complainers at the window. "Seem to be in a hurry to get themselves killed—or die trying."

"And Sleeping Beauty over there?"

"It's a damn shame some people just can't relax." He grinned. "Give him a kiss, Prince Charming, if you want his opinion on current events."

"Name's Hawk." I reached out to shake his hand.

"Jack." He held up his bleeding palm. "Got me a hell of a sliver.

"Too bad there ain't no Purple Hearts in Jungleland."

"Check."

The men at Eric's desk stood up and shook hands all around.

"Come on," the mercenary officer said wearily as he passed by on his way out.

The three complainers followed after him like eager puppies. The nodder woke up and looked around with a confused expression on his face as if he didn't quite know where he was.

He stood, stretched, then shuffled out the door.

"You want the honors?" Jack asked.

I shook my head.

"Suit yourself." He stood up, went over, and kicked the man on the bench hard in the ass. "Come on, Sleeping Beauty. Duty calls."

The man jerked around like a beached bass and rolled off the bench onto the floor hard.

Jack looked over at me and smiled. "I ain't no Prince Charming. Come on, sleepyhead."

Eric wandered over from his desk, leaving behind the nattily dressed officers. "Pleasant fellows. But…"

"But when you need a junkyard dog, you want a junkyard dog."

Eric just nodded.

"We need a junkyard dog?"

Eric nodded. "For now. They will be setting up a perimeter for us."

"What gives?"

"The Simbas have taken hostages. As many as twenty or thirty." He looked at me. "Missionaries and nuns, mainly. They're taking them north."

That explained the extra muscle Father Bob brought with him.

"And these guys?" I nodded towards the Belgian and his shadow.

"We all have our minders, now, don't we?" Eric sighed. "We'll give them a good show and send them off on their way, forthwith."

I looked over at the pair of Majors twisting their heads around aimlessly like turkeys scrounging for food.

"Good. Then, we'll get on with our business." Eric gave a

huff. "Did you get the valve for Sparks?"

I nodded. "He's working on Angel's plane."

"Yes, then." Eric looked down at me and squinted. "And…"

I patted my flight bag.

"Thank you. I, ah, appreciate it." He looked back at his minders. "I'll stop by your tent later."

Outside the Ferret and Jeep engines came to life. A grinding of gears announced their departure.

~~~

Makasi

Angel, Eduardo, and Rafael were parked at a table in the mess tent drinking coffee, probably complaining that it wasn't espresso.

The Cuban pilots were called Makasi, a Lingala word meaning strong and powerful. Their planes—our planes made what they called "the noise of final judgement," so the Makasi called them *El Enano que le ronca,* which meant either the dwarf that snores or the midget with big testicles, depending on who you asked.

They were all retreads from President Kennedy's Bay of Pigs fiasco who ended up exiled in Florida, until the 303 Committee at the C.I.A. decided to put them to use here in Jungleland, which they happily agreed to: if they couldn't fight back against Fidel himself, then giving his minders, the Russians and the Chinese, a bloody nose here in Africa was the next best thing. They were tough sons-of-bitches for sure. And damn good pilots.

"*Hola,* Hawk," Angel called out. "Sit. Sit, my friend."

I grabbed a cup of coffee and joined them. "So, what are you boys talking about?"

Angel looked at Eduardo, then Rafael. "Why?"

"Okay, why what?" I asked.

"We think we should use the bombs," said Eduardo.

"And the napalm. Yes, the napalm as well," said Rafael. "We want to kill them. Kill them all."

"The Simbas, right?" I asked with a wry smile.

"Yes. Yes, of course. The Simba rebels." Angel shook his head. "Aye-yi-yi. Do you believe this guy?"

"If we used the bombs and the napalm, we could wipe them out," said Eduardo. *"Absolutamente."*

"Well, maybe the bombs. But napalm? Boy, I don't know. That's dangerous stuff. You could hurt yourselves."

"See, they do not trust us," said Rafael. "Just like before."

"Before?" I asked.

"Bahía de Cochinos. In Cuba," said Angel. "How quickly they all forget."

"So, what's the matter with the rockets?" I asked.

"With the napalm, we could wipe them out," said Eduardo.

"Well, well, well…just look at what we have here," Roscoe said, sitting down beside me. "A regular Air Force kind of coffee klatch. Look at you guys with your bulls and everything. Very classy. So, where's yours?"

Alfalfa pointed at the empty space on my flight suit. The Cubans all had their black bull emblem hijacked from a local beer sewn over their hearts.

"Hey, yeah, *Mr. Hawk,"* said Angel. "Where is your bull?"

I shook my head. "That's your thing. I'm no Makasi."

"Don't sell yourself short, my friend," said Angel,

"We want to kill them," said Eduardo.

"Who? The Simbas?" asked Alfalfa.

"Aye-yi-yi," Angel moaned.

"We want to burn them up with the bombs and the napalm." Eduardo swooped his hand down over the table like an airplane. "Wipe them out."

"Napalm?" Roscoe shook his head. "You'll put your eye out."

"Put your eye out? What does that mean?" Rafael asked.

"I mean, it is dangerous stuff." Roscoe turned to me. "Don't you think?".

I shrugged. "They really, really want to kill them, you know?"

"No bombs. No napalm," said Roscoe. "Use your rockets and use your machine guns."

"See, they do not trust us," said Rafael. "Just like before."

"Look, I trust you. But the 303 Boys downtown, they're a different story." Roscoe looked around the table. "Anyway, it seems we've got some serious issues going on in Stanleyville."

"Eric told me there are a bunch of hostages being held there," I said.

"About three hundred total, we think. You know what they will do to them." Roscoe stared off into space.

"Then we will kill them," said Eduardo.

Alfalfa shook his head. He pointed my way with his finger and smiled. "So…did you ask him?"

"Oh, yes, yes, yes." Angel looked around the table at his cohorts. They all grinned at me like chimpanzees. "Tell us, my friend. Tell us."

"What?"

"*La roja,* of course."

"Dr. Mickelson?"

"Of course. Of course. In Elisabethville. What happened? Tell us everything. *Everything.*"

"The Big K," Roscoe said. "According to Ernie, he struck out big time. Right? Breakfast all by his lonesome. It's just so sad."

"It's a long season," I said.

"Well, at least you went down swinging." Alfalfa sighed and looked around the table. "That's what counts…*I suppose.*"

"Oh, my friend, my friend." Angel shook his head. "Well, if

you're not up to the job. I think I can be of some assistance."

"Or me," said Rafael.

"No, no. It is I," said Eduardo. "I know the ways of these women."

"I think I've got this under control," I said. "You guys can stand down already."

Alfalfa just smiled. "It's nice to have such good friends."

Angel gave me an evil grin.

"Given any thought to our conversation?" Roscoe asked.

"Some. Sounds like you had the same discussion with Sparks."

"He ain't no dummy."

"No. No, he's not."

"It'll all work out…I hope."

"So, what's with the Commando boys on our doorstep," I asked.

"Just a little insurance policy."

"Is this your doing, or…"

"I've got a little pull left—or I should say Uncle Sam does. If you know what I mean."

"You trying to make me feel all warm and fuzzy?"

"Maybe something like that." Roscoe looked me dead in the eye. "So, what's your plan?"

"I don't know." I looked at Angel, Eduardo, and Rafael. "Maybe kill some Simbas."

"Yes, we are with Hawk on this one," said Angel.

"That'll do for now," Roscoe said. "I guess."

~~~

The Mayor

It was long after dark. I lay on my bed staring at the ceiling and thinking about Ella, Father Bob, and Simon—then trying unsuccessfully not to.

"Hawk. Hawk, it's me."

I recognized Eric's voice outside. I wanted to roll over, but I also wanted his stash out of my tent. I lit my Coleman lantern. "Yeah. Come on in."

The flap opened, and Eric stepped in. "I'm sorry it's so late. I was—I'm, ah…Anyways."

He sat down in the canvas deck chair and leaned himself over.

I sat up on my cot and looked at him. He trembled ever so slightly. "You okay?"

"Yes, yes, I'm fine. I'm fine." Eric looked over my way, then quickly scanned around my tent. "Yeah, well, maybe not terribly so."

"I got your…" I reached under my bed and pulled his package out of my footlocker.

"Oh. Okay. Good, but…"

I offered the bag his way. "I don't really care, except—"

"Yes, yes, I understand." He took the bag and set it on his lap. He turned it over, then turned it back over again, patting it gently. His eyes scanned nervously.

"Eric."

He looked at me.

"What is wrong?"

"Do you know what they did?"

"Who is they?"

"The Simbas. Up north. In Stanleyville."

I shook my head.

He nodded his head quickly up and down. "You would not think that—you know, the cruelty of it all."

"What did they do?"

"Well, you know they have several hundred prisoners up there and they are threatening to kill them all if the government forces come."

"And we're going, right?"

"Oh, yes. Oh, yes. You will hear about it tomorrow."

"But what did they do?" I asked.

"The Simbas? They are—" He stood up.

"Eric." I stood up and grabbed his shoulder. "What is going on?"

Eric slowly sat back down. "It was the mayor."

"And?"

"And the mayor there, Bond…Bondess…Bondekwe or something. I don't know, but they stripped him down completely naked and stood him up in front of a mad, mad crowd of rebels."

I waited. "And?"

Eric shook his head.

"And?"

"And they carved his liver out—while he was still alive."

I could feel my face squint in repulsion.

"Yes, while he was still alive."

"Alive?"

"Then they cut it up while it was still hot and—and—and they ate it in front of him as he died."

I sat down at the end of my cot. "Jesus."

"Yes, damn it—Jesus Christ, already. Yes, right in front of him. While he watched them and died."

We sat in silence.

Eric rolled the wax paper package over and over in his lap.

I stared into the floor.

Eric suddenly took a deep breath and straightened up his spine. "Tomorrow."

I looked up at him. "Yeah, what? What happens tomorrow?"

Eric stood up quickly. "We are going to get those evil bastards. Once and for all."

I watched him turn and quickly leave my tent.

Outside, as he walked away, I heard him say, "Once and for all. Once and for all."

After a while, I lay back down and thought again about Ella.

~~~

Les Affreux

I slept, finally. Not well, but I did sleep some. It was still dark when I woke, thinking again of Ella.

I dressed in fatigues and a T-shirt. I strapped on my Colt. The mess tent was empty. Guys were in the back fixing breakfast. I got a quick cup of coffee, downed it, then moved on towards the flight line.

Sparks had put some nose art on my T-6, not the Makasi black bull, but a hunting hawk. It fit. Like old times. I walked around the plane, mindlessly checking the hinge points, vents, ports, and pitot tube. Angel's plane was back online, beside mine, ready to go. I leaned against the horizontal stabilizer and watched the sun appear quickly through the trees.

As soon as it was light, I headed to the runway and began jogging. It was five thousand feet or so. Sometimes PT helps clear the mind. Sometimes it misses the mark.

I ran down, crossed over the runway, and came back on the other side. I turned again. And headed back to the far end.

Scattered gunshots brought me up short when I got to the far threshold.

A quarter-mile off through the trees, I could make out the mercenary Ferret and Jeeps parked at the top of a rise. It looked like Sergeant Jack was there leaning against the front of the Jeep, smoking a cigarette.

I swung off to the left and found the road leading towards the village and jogged his way.

He saw me coming. He left his rifle leaning at his side and lit another cigarette.

I walked the last fifty yards towards him.

"Hawk. Out for a morning run, are we?"

"What's going on? I heard shooting."

"Eh, the boys are getting a little stir crazy." Jack looked halfway down the hill. "I told them it was just monkeys or something, but, you know, they had to go and find out for themselves."

Three of the mercenaries were gathered in a clearing down the hill.

One of them fired off a shot.

"What's he shooting at?" I asked.

"Take a look." Jack handed me a pair of binoculars.

I scanned the valley. "I don't see anything."

"Further out. About three hundred yards or so, I'd say."

I slowly worked the tree line back and forth, moving out slowly. I saw a clearing far below. I watched, then saw movement. "Those aren't monkeys—"

A shot rang out.

One of the tribesmen in the clearing fell.

Two of the mercenaries clapped the shooter on his back.

"Bad luck for him, I guess," Jack said.

"Who are they?"

"Don't know. Rebels? Bandits? Who cares?"

I looked at Jack.

"Whoever they are, they should probably keep their distance."

I handed the binoculars back.

Jungleland

Jack grinned. "You think?"
I just turned and jogged back to camp.

~~~

Kilometer 8

The operations Quonset hut was set up for a good, old-fashioned, *Twelve O'clock High,* official-type briefing. Up on the dais at the front of the room, Eric the Red consulted with the two dandies in uniforms so clean that they were no doubt fighting the war from trenches formed by Steelcase desks and file cabinets far behind the front lines. Hanging off to the side up front, Roscoe and a mercenary officer watched the room fill by dribs and drabs with the whole motley crew of our squadron—pilots, mechanics, line boys, and cooks—scattering themselves in the chairs facing the stage and the maps of Central Africa behind them. Alfalfa saw me. He gave me a wry smile and a three-fingered Boy Scout salute.

"So, what'd I miss?" I asked Angel as I sat down beside my wingman.

"Well, it looks like you are right. Rumor has it that our little corner of jungle paradise is going to become something of a total fustercluck—You know, for the Simbas."

"Oh, yeah? What's today's special? FUBAR casserole?"

"Something like that." Angel turned and looked me up and down. He gave me an evil smile.

"What?" I asked.

He leaned in. "Come on now. It is just you and I, right now."

"Yeah. And?"

He whispered. *"Médica."*

"The Doc?"

"Come on. You can tell me. *Trust me.*"

I sighed.

"I could use a happy story."

I gave an apathetic half-shrug. "We knocked back a few beers at Ernie's Place. That's all."

"A date date?"

"Burgers and beers after a long day at work." I looked at Angel. "She lost her patient. Not a good day."

"My condolences. Maybe next time—*if there is a next time.*"

I shrugged.

"For you, that is." Angel flashed a devilish grin. *"Maybe…"*

"Yeah. Right," I said and thought, *As if.*

Sparks found me and sat down. *"Idiots."*

"Morning, sunshine," I said.

"Why do I have to be here? Huh?"

At the front of the room, Eric and the uniforms straightened up from their consult, ready to brief us.

"All right, then, men," Eric called out in his clipped British accent and surveyed the room, waiting for the conversation to fade out. He tapped one of the easels with his pointer until the room quieted down. "In case you haven't already heard, we've got something of a situation brewing up north that we've been asked to lend some assistance in resolving."

Angel poked my ribs with his elbow. "Told you."

Eric turned to the huge map on the wall behind him and slapped it loudly with the wooden pointer he had been holding to the side of his leg.

"Here. East Southeast of Stanleyville. Approximately

battalion strength, correct?" Eric turned to the Belgian Army officer, who confirmed with a sharp nod of his head.

A long, low whistle was heard in the room.

"Exactly. This, by the way, is Major Blume of the Belgian Army. And this is Major Lokombe of the *Armée Nationale Congolaise.*"

"They do love their uniforms, don't they," Angel whispered to me.

"Major Blume, perhaps you could give the men an overview of this action?"

Eric stepped back, and Major Blume rose. He tugged at the sleeves of his neatly pressed blouse.

"Yes. Of course. As you all know, a group calling itself the People's Republic of the Congo, led by Christopher Gbenye, has taken Stanleyville with the support of the Soviet Union and their African proxies. They are holding two or three hundred hostages in the city itself and another twenty-five to fifty at an outpost eight kilometers away." Blume looked at Eric, then turned back to us. "There have been reports coming to us of…atrocities, if you will."

Eric looked directly at me and nodded.

I shook my head and whispered to Angel, "Yup, a good, old-fashioned Charlie Foxtrot going on up there."

"Our plan is called Dragon Rouge. We will drop Belgian paratroopers in on the Stanleyville airport, using American C-130s," Blume continued in his French accent. "In support of that landing, we will have three Commando Groups moving north starting tomorrow. You will be helping to clear their way to the city and then attack the Simba forces in the area. We need to move as quickly as possible to save the hostages."

Major Blume looked around the room.

Roscoe closed his eyes and shook his head. He looked at me and gave me a half-smile.

Blume sat down.

Eric stepped forward. "Major Lokomba? Do you have anything to add?"

Lokomba looked around the room and shook his head.

"Very well," Eric said, stepping close to the maps. "Commando 5, Commando 6, and Commando 10 will all be moving simultaneously into Stanleyville. Commandos 6 and 10—located to the east here, along the mountains—will be moving north by these routes here. They will be supported by flights out of Albertville. Here. And here."

Eric drew two separate lines up roads along the mountains, then across on RN3 with his pointer.

"How many vehicles will Commando 5 have?" Eric asked.

"Sixty. About three hundred men," said the mercenary officer. "We will split into three groups. Commando 51 will approach from the east from Bukavo. Commandos 52 and 53 will approach the city from the west."

"Okay, Angel, Hawk, Eduardo, and Rafael, you will take the western contingent along this route, here. Mario, Luis, Antonio, and César you will cover further to the east. We will fly staggered sorties to maintain constant air cover. Any questions?" Eric stared around the room. "We—we need to get these guys north as quickly as possible and then to pound those Simba assets around Kilometer 8 for their advance."

Silence from the group.

"Major Blume? Do you have anything more?"

He shook his head. "No."

Jungleland

"Roscoe?"

Alfalfa stepped forward along the side of the dais.

"These are not hit-and-run guerrillas. They've been armed and trained by the Russians and have shown some organization and discipline in executing their movements and engagements. No real evidence of anti-aircraft artillery, but they do have fifty-caliber weapons and some twenty and thirty-seven mike-mikes mounted on pickup trucks. So, be careful. Oh, and, whatever you do, don't get shot down and captured. We all know what they do to POWs."

Alfalfa stepped back.

The room was quiet.

"Right." Eric took center stage again. "Very well. We will meet at oh-five-thirty tomorrow to pick up your map packets and go over the final details. Get some rest."

The group began fraying as pilots stood up and started drifting out of the building.

Alfalfa wandered down to meet me. "The doc?"

"Headed back home with the Padre…and Simon. You know him?"

"Yeah. Yeah, I do."

"And?"

"Pay for play. As long as the money is rolling in…I guess they'll be okay."

"If not?"

"Well, I don't think he's too fond of the Simbas, but he doesn't trust the ANC either. Kind of an independent S.O.B."

"I get it."

"Here, give this to Father Bob." Roscoe pulled an envelope from his back pocket and handed it to me. "Maybe it will help out a bit with the Simon thing. Just in case."

"Will do."

The C.I.A man frowned. He jerked his head towards the maps on the wall. "Serious business, Hawk. Be careful."

"Always, Alfalfa. Always." I began to turn away.

Roscoe grabbed my shoulder. "I'm serious. Just remember, this isn't Europe. If you get shot down, there's no place to hide from the rebels with that pasty white face of yours."

It brought me up short. I hadn't thought about that.

Roscoe gently slapped my cheek. He smiled, then headed out.

~~~

Kaffirs and Mondele

"Going for a ride, are we now?" asked Sergeant Jack as I pulled up to the mercenary outpost beyond the wire.

I slowed my Jeep and stopped. "Just a walk in the park."

"I suppose it might be a fine enough day." Jack grinned. "All by your lonesome, though, eh?"

"Made the ride before. I've got some meds to deliver." *Not to mention Alfalfa's pile of money.* "I'll be back before dark."

"Yeah. That'd be best." Jack looked down the hill. "We wouldn't want any friendly-fire type incidents."

"Yeah. I got it."

"And make a lot of noise, why don't you."

"How's that?"

"The kaffirs. They hate it, you know?"

I put the Jeep in first gear.

"Anyways, you have a wonderful day."

I was going to ask but decided not to. I let the clutch out and headed into the dark tunnel of the jungle.

~ ~ ~

The ride to the mission was uneventful—until I got to the last road into the village. There was a telephone pole laid across two fifty-five gallon drums: a standard-issue African roadblock.

I slowed and stopped. Two men dressed in khakis and white shirts carrying AK-47 rifles stepped out on the other side.

"Mondele! Mondele!," one called out.

I gripped the wheel hard to keep my hands there. "I am going to the mission. I've got medicine."

The second man raised his rifle.

"Ask Father Bob. He knows me."

A moment later, Simon stepped out from behind the men. He casually walked around the barricade and came over beside me in the Jeep.

"You…you took my man to the hospital." His voice was low and soothing. He looked down at me and smiled. "On the airplane. With the doctor."

I nodded. "I, ah—it was all I could do."

He rested his palms on the pistols in his holster.

"I'm sorry."

Simon stared at my FN FAL rifle laying between the front seats, then looked back at me. He smiled. "This one will be okay. Let him pass by."

The two men looked up at the tall man. He nodded.

They slid the telephone pole aside.

Simon stepped closer. He lowered his voice. "You should know, not everyone is welcome out here."

"Do you work for Father Bob?"

"Sometimes."

I looked back up at him.

"Today, I do. Tomorrow…" He looked down the road towards the village. Turning back to me, he shrugged. "Who knows what will happen then?"

"But today, you are watching out for Father Bob and Dr.

Mickelson.”

"I suppose I am.”

"Thank you.”

"You know, up in your aeroplane, in the sky, you are safe. Down here, you cannot hide so much.” He rubbed his cheek. "Do you know what I mean?”

"I do.”

"Your friends, *the white giants,* they are not so very nice. Do you know?”

I thought of Jack's mercenaries shooting the men down the hill. I nodded again.

"Remember this, then.” He gave me a broad, toothy smile. "You may go now.”

I tried to smile back. "Thanks.”

Simon stepped back, and I drove through. They closed the roadblock behind me.

~~~

Father Bob heard the Jeep and stood in the door of his parsonage. He had a serious look on his face. A man sitting outside beside the door stood and grabbed for his rifle.

I slowed down, then stopped in front of him. The streets were empty: no kids.

"Well, I am surprised to see you here again so soon.” Father Bob motioned for Simon's man to sit back down. He came down beside the Jeep. "You met some of my other men out on the road, I take it. Did you see Simon?”

"He was there. At the roadblock.”

"Good.” He looked down the road I came in on.

"Sometimes…"

I didn't want to ask but did, "Where's Ella?"

"Down in the village. People are strange any more. They don't want to come by. So, she goes to them."

I wondered if Jack's men shot some of the tribesmen. "Anyway, I've got meds."

"Okay. Good."

I sighed. I pulled Alfalfa's money out of my pocket. "And maybe this could come in handy, too."

Father Bob stared for a moment at my hand. "Roscoe Pettis?"

I nodded.

He took the envelope, opened it, and slowly flipped through the thick stack of twenty-dollar bills.

"Take it. He doesn't care. It's not out of his pocket."

Father Bob nodded slowly.

"Use it to pay Simon."

"We are okay for now. But, maybe…" He sighed and pushed the envelope into his pants pocket. "They are closer now. To the northwest, they tell me."

I thought of Alfalfa's plan to have a plan. "So, what now?"

Father Bob shrugged. "We work, I guess. As best as we can."

"You and Ella could come back to the base."

He shook his head.

"For a little while."

"No. No, that will not work. You know how it is. The people would never trust us. Especially now with the mercenaries there."

"You know that, too?"

"Simon told us."

I wanted to plead but did not. Suddenly, the jungle seemed even taller…darker. I reached between the seats and pulled out a bottle of scotch. "Might be the last of this I bring by for a while."

"Why is that?"

"Our operations will be picking up some."

"Up to the north?"

I nodded. "Stanleyville."

"We've heard about that, too. The villagers know more than us. The drums tell them. It is bad?"

"Yeah. Yeah, it is."

"Well, then, maybe Roscoe's offering will come in handy." He patted the money in his pocket. "And when this mess is all over, we can break bread again."

"Good." I looked towards the village huts down the way.

"You should go see her." Father Bob leaned in to pick up the boxes of medicine. "Just leave the Jeep here."

I nodded. I grabbed my rifle, threw it over my shoulder, and headed towards the collection of grass huts a quarter-mile down the road.

The tunnel through the triple canopy went strangely quiet as I passed. As I approached the village, mothers noticed me and called to their children to bring them inside. I stopped just outside the edge of the first row of huts. Fearful mother's faces were replaced with the hard-set glares of men peering out from the doorways and staring from between the huts.

Three or four huts in, I saw one of Simon's men sitting on the ground, cradling his AK-47 against his forehead.

I looked back at the men in the doorways.

Ella stepped out of the hut, carrying a doctor's bag. A young woman followed her out. Ella leaned in to speak into the woman's ear. Ella rubbed her arm, then wrapped it around her neck to hug her gently.

I waited.

Ella released the woman and patted her shoulder.

Simon's man stood. He saw me and raised his rifle.

Ella noticed, then looked my way. She pushed the rifle barrel back down.

Some of the men stepped out from between the huts, still staring at me.

Ella walked towards me. She looked into the eyes of the tribesmen as she passed. Simon's man followed close behind.

"Hmm, what brings you to town, stranger?" she asked, stepping up to me.

"I, ah, dropped off some meds." The tribesmen had stepped in closer. "And Father Bob said to come down and say hi."

"Well, I am working here." Ella smiled as she looked around again. She motioned for Simon's man to stay, then grabbed my arm and led me back the way I came a bit for privacy. "There's been some shootings. I need to take care of them."

"That explains the welcome wagon."

"Are you staying for dinner?"

"I can't. I have to get back."

"Well, I'm sorry."

"Yeah. Me, too."

She smiled.

"You know, right? About what is going on?"

"We've heard some things. I always have one of Simon's men with me now. We should be alright. What about you?"

"We'll be flying again in the morning. Pushing north to Stanleyville. You know."

"You are going to save those people?"

"I'll be helping out, as best as I can." I took a deep breath. "You don't think it might be better for you and Bob to work out of the base? For a little while?"

She shook her head. "They need me here. Not there."

"I get it, but…"

"We'll be fine."

I took her gently by the arm and led her away a bit. I reached into my pocket and pulled out a thousand dollars I had rolled up in a wad. "Here. Take this."

"For what?"

"I gave some to Bob, too. Keep it safe and use it for Simon if you need it."

She looked at the cash.

I slid it inside her doctor's bag. "Or use it to make your way out of here. If it comes to that."

"Hawk—"

"I won't be back for a while. At least a week or so. Maybe more. If you don't need it, buy some licorice for the kids."

"You'll be back, right?

I looked at Simon's man and the tribesmen. "I'll be okay. Just take care of yourself and Father Bob."

"Hawk…" Ella stepped up and gave me a hug. "I've got to, you know…"

"Yeah, go help people."

She nodded.

I watched her walk back into the village, then headed back to my Jeep.

~~~

Father Bob waved at me from the doorway.

I drove back the way I came in. Simon must have heard me coming back. He had the gate opened and was leaning casually on the empty barrel.

I slowed and stopped. We stared. "You'll take care of them, right?"

Simon smiled. "I will do what I can, of course."

"I…" *What could I say?*

"She called you the Hawkman."

"Just Hawk, really."

"Yes. Yes, I like that one, I think." Simon pursed his lips. "You might not want to come back…for a little while, anyway. Do you know what I mean?"

I nodded, then drove off.

✳✳✳~~~✳✳✳

The Caterpillar Club

The next morning we were up early and in the briefing room—just the pilots this time. Sparks and his guys were out prepping the planes. I guess the big briefing yesterday was just a show for the guys in the crisply pressed uniforms.

Nobody was up on the stage. Eric had a map laid out on a table, and we gathered around as he showed us the routes Commandos 52 and 53 would be taking towards Stanleyville. He drew a couple of bold red lines along narrow, winding jungle roads coming into Stanleyville from the west.

"We don't know where exactly the Simbas will be. But we can suspect that there will be certain pinch zones—here, and here and here," Eric said, circling a half-dozen areas along the routes. "Watch these spots closely. Especially the ones up along the river, here. Got it?"

Everybody just stared at the maps.

"Like Roscoe said yesterday, the rebels have been getting better. They've got Russian and Chinese rifles, along with machine guns, mortars, and some of them have cannons—especially the closer you get to Stanleyville. So, be careful." Eric stood up from the table. "We need to get the Commandos there as quickly as possible so they can be on the scene when the Belgians drop on the airport. We've got five days to get it done. Right?"

"We will take care of it," said Angel.

"Yes, we will wipe them out," Eduardo said.

"Good." Eric nodded. "We will fly staggered sorties to maintain constant air cover over the troops. Angel, Eduardo, Rafael, and Hawk, you will be in the first group covering this route. Antonio, Luis, Juan, and Mario, you will be working Commando 52 along this area down here. There are maps in your packets."

"Don't worry, Eric," I said. "We'll get those guys up there."

"Good." Eric exhaled loudly.

As we headed to the door, Angel asked me, "Do you want the lead?"

I had not thought about it as my mind wandered off to Ella at the mission in the jungle. "You take it. I'll get my turn."

"You are a real pal."

I noticed Roscoe in the back of the room. I stopped on my way out. "Alfalfa…"

"How is she doing?" he asked.

"I saw her yesterday. Looking after her patients, I guess."

Roscoe had a pained look on his face.

"What?"

"This whole situation is going to stir things up like a Waring blender."

"You think she's in danger?"

"Be a hell of a lot better if she and Father Bob were in Leo or E'ville."

"You know that's not going to happen. I tried. I tried to get them to come here just for a little bit. But no."

"Yeah. I kind of figured."

"At least they've got Simon on their side."

He nodded. "As long as the cash is there for him."

"And what about you?"

"They want me down in Kamina getting the troopers all set on the C-130s."

"It's a big party."

"The biggest. Then they'll send me into Stanleyville. To clean up the mess." Roscoe shrugged. "It keeps me busy, I guess."

"Semper fi."

"Yeah. Break a leg."

I nodded, then headed out to the tarmac.

*****~~~*****

I lost myself in my checklist, mindlessly pushing through it, going over every damn rivet and trying to get Ella out of my head. I double-checked the ammo bins were locked down and the rocket pods were all filled.

As I was strapping in, Angel started his engine. I cranked mine over. Soon the engine oil temperature was up, and we taxied out to begin our day.

The column was to the north. Angel led. I followed until we passed the muster point. He dove and buzzed the column. No worries about enemy aircraft from the Simbas.

They were already moving to the east, and we spread out on either side of the road, flying five miles out, then ranging back in. Out and back. Out and back. Not much happened in the early going. So, we burned off our fuel, traded off with Eduardo and Rafael, then headed back to the base to top off again.

Coming back on station, the Makasi were pounding a rebel ambush site. Angel and I hung back until they had made their passes, then we went in.

Angel took the lead and stitched up the jungle on the right side of the road. I followed on the left.

Angel came back in and unloaded his rockets.

I followed with more machine guns, lacing up the jungle canopy where most of the tracers came from. I saw a pickup truck with .50 caliber machine guns firing away. I arced right and cut into him with my machine guns, then pulled left.

The Ferrets rolled up and engaged.

To the northwest, I could see enemy pickups moving forward. Their tracers lit into the Commandos. I put my right wing on the ground and pirouetted two hundred and seventy degrees around and unloaded my rockets. I saw the first ones hit on target then climbed straight out over the explosions.

And then the fight was suddenly over.

The Simbas disappeared into the jungle.

The mercenaries pulled up and searched the area quickly. As I circled back, I noticed the Commandos firing down at the ground, then turned east to check the road ahead.

We waited for our replacements, then made one last trip for more fuel and ammo once Eduardo and Rafael were back.

We had one more round to go before night fell.

The Commandos made nearly fifty kilometers that day before we quit. It was only going to get harder the further north they pushed.

I slept well that night.

*** ~ ~ ~ ***

And the next day was the same. We met again with Eric, but it was the same briefing. The same issues. The same concerns. Just a little bit closer to the city. We knew the Commandos would be pushing into harder territory. There would be more rebels. With more equipment aiming our way.

Me? I just wanted to be up top again where it was cooler.

I walked around the plane, checking the static ports, the pitot tube, the engine, and, of course, the rockets and machine guns. Good to go. Then we waited until Eduardo and Rafael radioed they would be on their way back soon. We got in, fired up, and took off.

Angel gave me the lead, and we headed up the road towards Stanleyville. We found the column and swung up the narrow ribbon of red mud cutting in and out of the jungle canopy. I took the east side; Angel took the west. We throttled back to do our Kit Carson of the route ahead of the convoy.

The road wound along the jungle, disappearing into the canopy, then coming back out again. To the east, peaks rose up. We came to the river. Angel veered west, and I turned to the east, looking for the rebels. No telltale signs, yet.

We turned southwest. By the time we got back to the column, they were moving again. We climbed a thousand feet higher to get a better look down through the treetops and headed to the east again.

The cool air felt good, though the sun shone into the cockpit. I could feel the warmth starting to come out of me. It would keep getting hotter again as the day went on.

We circled back and began a two- or three-mile-long race track course over the road in advance of the column. I flew out ahead. Angel lagged behind on his side. We stayed quiet on the radio, though no one would miss the sounds of our engines.

We were coming up on the river again, ahead of the column

by a couple of miles or so.

"Do you see?" Angel radioed.

"Negative."

He accelerated by me, climbed, then rolled off to turn back. I turned and followed.

"Where are you, my friends? Where are you?" Angel said over the radio as he rolled back down on the road below five hundred feet.

I saw nothing to either side.

Angel dumped a pair of rockets into the far side of the river. They disappeared into the treetops. Seconds later they erupted. It didn't take long until the red and green blossoms of tracer bullets launched up on his tail.

I angled around on the near shore and sprayed the area with machine-gun fire.

Angel faked right and turned south.

I did not see the emplacements but worked the ground with fire.

Turning north, I saw the column moving our way. I radioed home for Eduardo and Rafael to head up our way.

Angel went high. I stayed low, skimming the top canopy, too close for small arms. Prop full RPM. Throttle to thirty-two. I swung wide to give him space to come around again from the south. The trees were a blur. I was in and out of the late morning mist.

Looking up, I saw Angel's T-6 pull an Immelmann. He rolled right-side up and loitered for just a moment, then dove straight down on the emplacements from above.

I rolled southwest, then west. As he came in, I turned back north again. There were now more than just light arms. I could see fifty-caliber and some cannon fire coming on his tail.

Angel's rockets came down hard. He rolled out to the south.

I stayed low, coming around to the north where they'd have little time to aim. Turning on line, I climbed to give me altitude for my rockets, then let loose with all twelve, diving down to a couple hundred feet. I figured I could come back with machine guns a couple of times, then Eduardo and Rafael would be there.

I could not hear, but I could feel the 7.62 bullets hit my wings. I didn't see it fire, the cannon, that is. My right wing arced up. I fought it back down and saw, as I climbed out, avgas misting out of a hole through my right wing.

She was done.

I maxed the throttle to forty and turned southwest towards home.

I knew I would not make it back.

I rolled inverted and climbed.

The canopy slid open. I wanted as much altitude as possible.

I couldn't wait. I had two thousand feet. I couldn't wait.

Near vertical, I loosened my belt and began to slide out. Kicking the stick forward, the plane climbed up and away.

And I was thrown out.

Five seconds later, I pulled. The harness nearly knocked my breath away. I made the Club.

And I was floating down into the jungle canopy, under the silk.

~~~

Jungleland

Thrown into the slipstream the air was cold. It beat my eyes closed. And then it was calm again. And as I floated down, the heat and humidity grabbed at me.

I opened my eyes and looked over my shoulder. The T-6 arced up and over. The wing caught fire. As the plane came down, it collapsed in on itself and tumbled indelicately out of control toward the ground. I did not see the final fall, just the smoke.

I looked down, searching for an opening in the tall treetops. I steered to the left. It's not the fall, but the landing that gets you hurt. If my chute held, it would still be a hundred and fifty feet down to the ground. It had been a long, long time since I had jumped.

A moment of peace, falling. Still flying, somewhat.

I pulled my legs in and crashed through a gap in the top layer of leaves. My silk caught the branches up top. I could feel my chute collapsing.

I reached out at the tree limbs on my way down, pulling off leaves and branches.

Half-collapsed, my speed increased until I hit the second layer and grabbed the top of a banana tree and held. I was still up fifteen or twenty feet. The tree stood for a moment, then arced slowly down.

Fortunately, my parachute collapsed and fell freely. I could feel myself accelerating, but held on and rode the tree down to the ground through the vines until the slam of the jungle floor crushed the breath out of my body.

I rolled, gasping for air, and slid off the tree into a bed of wet ferns on the ground, covered with branches and bananas.

Overhead, Angel flew by, fast.

I lay silent. Trying to catch my breath. I was afraid to try to move. Afraid for the pain to come back to me. My legs ached, but I could move them. My arms automatically went up to my head and snatched off my helmet. It was heavily scarred from a tree branch. I didn't even feel it coming down.

I looked up and saw my chute floating easily down through the hole I left. It was held up in a small stand of low trees.

My breathing slowly came back to normal. I closed my eyes and took a few deep breaths, then decided to sit up.

Angel or Eduardo or Mario flew over the top again. I could not see who it was.

I turned and leaned back against the tree trunk. I was surprised my back didn't hurt. The fall through the jungle happened so fast, there wasn't even time to tense up.

Without thinking, my hands started unbuckling my parachute harness. Then I was on my feet, pulling it down out of the trees. I gathered it up and buried it as best as I could under the banana tree, ripping off fern leaves to cover it up.

My 1911 was under my left arm. I had two more magazines beneath my right.

I found the compass in my pants pocket. It was still intact. Where the hell was I?

I had to get moving…quickly. But where?

I sat on the downed tree trunk and thought. Where was the

river?

I looked through the bunches of banana on the ground to find a ripe one and pealed it to eat. Slowly the taste came through. It might have been a plantain. Alfalfa said they're better for you. More starch—whatever. It tasted good.

Where was the river? I needed to find it and move back upstream towards the base.

I closed my eyes and recalled the last of the rockets coming off the plane. The lifting release of weight. Pulling out, feeling the AK-47s hitting me, then fighting the wing back down after the cannon hit. Seeing the damage and arcing up and back to the southwest.

Where was the river? Did I cross it again coming back?

I did not know. But I needed to move.

Southwest looked good. Home was that way.

There's no Geneva Convention in *Jungleland*.

I pocketed a half-dozen ripe plantains and headed that way.

And now the race began.

~~~

Escape and Evasion

It had been a damn long time, like a decade and a half, since I sat through an Escape and Evasion briefing back in England—not that finding my way to Holland or Belgium or Spain would be of much help to me now.

The T-6s crossed overhead, but even if they could get a chopper out to me today—and that was Roscoe's promise to us all, that he would save us—how could they get me out? I needed a place where they could land and pick me up.

The jungle was dark, twilight under the triple canopy in the middle of the day. No need for sunglasses. Wherever it was I was going to get to, I had to move fast for now.

Heading southwest, I worked quickly through the underbrush in the canopy opening I came down through, pushing through shrubs and ferns and yanking off the vines. I wasn't quiet—for now. I needed most of all to put some distance between myself and where I went down as quickly as possible.

The vegetation clawed back at me. At least there were no paths, which is good. No people around. I moved for thirty minutes or maybe an hour, then stopped on the downside of a hill and hunkered in.

I don't know how far I had gotten. Maybe a half-mile or so. I was hoping more, but it was very slow going. Hungry, I resisted the urge to eat again. I might need the plantains later.

Remembering what Roscoe told me from his days in Southeast Asia, I needed to slow down and start moving very quietly. I knew the jungle would become even darker soon. Midnight under a new moon—and without any headlights on the Jeep. Alfalfa said the dark would be good for me. If you can't see, then, remember, neither can they. And if someone is close and looking for you, then keep off the trail and stay put. Don't make any noise for them to find you.

I closed my eyes and listened like he said. After twenty minutes or so, the jungle sounds came back: the droning of insects mostly.

Birds cackled here and there. A low whistling and a crow squawk—no, probably a parrot. I heard scurrying at the treetops and a harsh, growling bark. Probably colobus monkeys. It was the quiet that told you someone was out there shutting nature down. Always listen for what you don't hear.

Curtains of gray moss, and creepers and lianas, hung down in tangles from the trees. The ferns were heavy with dew, even in the middle of the afternoon. The crush of humidity bore down on me, and I noticed myself sweating.

I played it over again and again in my head. Firing my rockets. The thunking pangs of small arms against the fuselage. Climbing—yanked hard to the left. The gaping hole in my wing. Clawing up at full power.

I think I was heading southwest. Where was the river?

Releasing the canopy. Grasping at my five-point harness. Sliding. Kicking the stick and throwing myself out of the cockpit. The T-6 cartwheeling in flames. Crashing through the trees. Floating into the jungle. That's where it ended.

Which way was I headed when I came down?

Suddenly the adrenalin rush was over. Even if I wanted to

move, I don't think I could. I lay my head back against the banana tree and closed my eyes. It would be just a moment, then I could move on.

When I woke, it was dark-dark. I could not see my hands in front of my face. Just like Roscoe said.

I listened. The droning buzz of cicadas rose in my ears. I heard bullfrogs—if they have those here. Far off, a low growl. Good.

I grabbed a plantain and ate. I listened. Then I slept again.

✳✳✳~~~✳✳✳

Early morning sunlight careened in between the treetops. I could see the vague outline of my hand.

The air chattered with bird songs and calls. I never noticed them before—the whistles and the caws and…chicken-like sounds.

A mosquito buzzed my ear, and I slapped it away. I kicked away ants crawling over my boots.

Then I remembered more. Roscoe said to watch your feet always. Always look before you step. After ten or fifteen minutes, stop. Wait and listen some more. Listen for the birds and insects and monkeys. Then, remember to move back on yourself the way you came.

"Buttonhook," Alfalfa called it. *You want to know if someone is behind you.*

I could see three or four feet. Then in a half-hour another five feet. It was time to move.

The river had to be the best place for a helicopter to get down to pick me up.

I stood up and moved. Gently stepping down and around the

vines and ferns.

I moved out slow like I was supposed to. Maddeningly slow. Much quieter now.

I checked my watch and made a note when to stop. I found a darker little corner in the jungle. I checked my watch and waited for fifteen minutes.

I listened again. Then, I heard it. Far off. I checked my compass: to the southwest. It sounded like a stream.

I moved on that way, then remembered the button hook. I'd try that next time.

Fifteen minutes later, I stopped and waited again. The jungle sounded the same, so I moved on. Ten minutes in, I turned back around to the left and moved halfway back the way I came, then hunkered.

Nothing. Birds. Insects. The humidity.

I checked my compass. I didn't know how far I had moved, but it seemed the water was a little bit louder. If I could find the stream, maybe I could follow it down to the river.

I curled back to the southwest again and moved forward, step-by-step.

I button hooked around to the right. I waited.

It would take forever to find the damned river.

How would they know where I am when I get there?

Talking Drums

I stopped. The jungle sounded the same. Cicadas. Bird songs. But something more. Off in the distance.

A faint humming it seemed. Off to the west. Maybe northwest.

This was the area where I flew Roscoe in the Bird Dog. He was scouting the route east to Stanleyville. I should have paid more attention. Too late now.

It seemed too soon, but I ate another plantain. The far humming was answered, louder this time. Closer. In the direction, I was headed. Drums.

It had to be by the river. But how far was it? I looked all around. If you can't see ten feet ahead, it could be anywhere.

I closed my eyes.

I listened.

The rhythm and tones of the drum modulated seductively. Then stopped.

Insects and birds.

If I could hear them, they had to be close.

I moved slowly and quietly in the direction of the drums.

I lost count of the buttonhooks—left, then right, then back to the left, again and again—leading into the afternoon.

I stopped again and listened.

Suddenly…*quiet.*

I froze.

I could hear a mumble, a low hum. Musical, like the drums.

Stay still. Stay quiet. That's what Roscoe said.

How close? In the jungle, everything seems close.

I closed my eyes.

Soon I could make out voices. Moving my way.

I could feel myself breathing harder and harder—could not help myself. I pushed back through the vines, deeper into the bush.

How many voices? I could not tell.

Several, it seemed. I did not know what they were saying. Their low, musical tone grew louder.

I wanted to believe I was invisible. Like Roscoe said. That they would walk by, but the voices grew louder,

I dug in.

Were they on a nearby trail?

Would they walk right into me? Or pass me by?

My breathing was labored. I tried to control it. I could hear it myself.

My watch said 2:43.

If it were night, I knew I'd be okay. They'd never see me.

The voices got louder. Close enough to tell now they were definitely to the Northwest.

Could I move?

I gripped my pistol. If I fired and ran, would it scare them enough to make them run?

Like Sergeant Jack said, *make a lot of noise and scare them off.*

But if they were rebels, they'd be armed. I did not need a gunfight.

I closed my eyes and put my forehead on my arms.

Trying to control my breathing.

Jungleland

The voices got closer. Their tone seemed hushed. There seemed to be three. Maybe four.

My watch said 3:07.

The jungle was quiet.

Damn it.

I drew my pistol. I moved slowly to the southwest again. Towards the river. Away from them.

If I waited…if they found me…if they stepped on me, it would be over.

Moving slowly, carefully watching to keep from making any noise at all.

I kept low. The moist earth absorbed my steps.

The voices grew louder still.

The low branches grabbed at my arms and legs in a slow-motion way. I quietly released myself as I moved away.

I prayed the dim twilight of the jungle floor would keep me hidden. I could see maybe five feet or more.

Stopping to listen. I couldn't tell if the voices were closer or not. Was it Swahili or Bantu or Lingala? I could not tell. It did not matter.

I looked: My watch said 3:18.

If I could keep them from coming closer…How far have I gone?

A deep breath. In through the nose. Slowly out from my mouth.

I moved.

Watching the jungle floor, I stepped carefully, on and on and on.

A parrot screeched, then flew away. I stopped and looked over my shoulder.

The voices fell quiet.

A long, tense silence.

One voice spoke. Softer now. I could barely hear it.

We all listened.

Another answered.

Listening.

Two or three spoke again. Louder. They seemed to be moving again.

Still looking back, I pressed forward. One step. Then beneath my foot, a branch cracked, and I froze.

Damn it.

I aimed my pistol to the northeast and fired a couple of times, hoping to send them that way, then moved quickly through the brush, still pushing ahead as quiet as I could, hoping to keep them off of me.

The reports died quickly, absorbed by the dense vegetation. An urgency rose in the voices.

I moved faster, thrashing now through the jungle.

The voices were louder, sharper, harsher.

The vines grabbed at my legs as I clawed harder through the brush.

I could not tell if the voices were following me or not.

I skittered like a pinball off the small tree trunks and low shrubs.

Pushing as hard as I could to get to the river—until the earth fell away.

I tumbled down a low ravine and through the muck on the floor of the jungle, slamming against the hard floor.

Dizzy. Shaking my head to clear the cobwebs.

How long had I been out?

Jungleland

I rose and grabbed at the branches on the other side to climb up.

When I got to the top, my head was bashed, and I fell backwards, losing consciousness.

~~~

A Poulet

My head pounded. Eyes pinched shut, hard. Arms bound behind my back.

A deep breath. I was curled in a ball.

It seemed dim. I slowly opened my eyes. The room was dark…and quiet. A small round hut.

I closed my eyes and tried not to move my aching head.

Guess it was a dumb move to try to outrun them. I remember shooting, running, then falling. Climbing, then, nothing more.

I lay for a long, long time, trying to absorb the darkness into my skull. Trying not to think about dumb mistakes. This one was a bad one. What would they do to me? Nothing pleasant, I was sure.

I listened again to the jungle. It slowly came alive again with the birds percolating in the trees.

I opened my eyes, and soft, pink light reflected off the back wall of the hut. I rolled slowly onto my back and stared at the thatched roof.

Outside, voices joined the birds, mostly from far away. Shuffling feet padded in the distance, then closer. Then away again.

I heard men speaking, softly then louder. Coming nearer and nearer.

Two men speaking in melodious tones. A third, his voice

deeper, answering shortly, curtly.

Outside the door, the conversation went on and on.

I closed my eyes again. I listened, not understanding a word, but fearing the worst.

The door opened and bathed me in a beam of harsh light. I spun away.

Two men grabbed my arms and pulled me out of the hut.

My head pounded. I looked down and away from the sun.

They pulled my head up by the hair on the back of my head. My temples throbbed. Even with my eyes closed, the sun pinched my eyelids tight.

Someone rubbed my face with their hand. A long, long speech I did not understand.

I opened my eyes. A crowd of bare-chested men gathered around me.

A man slapped my face and pointed at my chest. I stared at him, then turned to the man he was speaking to.

Simon smiled at me, listening to the man and nodding slowly.

He let the man go on and on. The other tribesmen pitched in with grunts and groans. The chief's arms flew around. He scowled at me, and I couldn't look away when I saw his teeth were sharpened into fine points. Finally, he ran out of words.

"These people, here…" Simon said politely to me, "They do not seem to like you so much."

"Mondele," said the angry man. He pushed my chest hard, back down into the men holding my arms. *Mondele.*"

The men stood me up again.

"Yes, yes…Mondele," Simon agreed.

I noticed a half-dozen of Simon's men in fatigues and t-shirts with rifles standing behind him. He spoke to one in Swahili. The man left.

"You know, Mr. Hawk, sometimes these people do some very unpleasant things when they are not happy," Simon said. He smiled a big toothy grin. "I think you can imagine."

I started to say something.

Simon put a finger up to his lips to stop me. He shook his head. *"Very unpleasant."*

Simon asked the man a question and got a long answer.

He nodded. "Did you blow up their chickens?"

I felt myself give a half-smile, then shook my head. "I did not know that they had any chickens."

Simon grinned back at me.

The man started to argue again, but Simon shut him down, putting his hand into his face.

"They do not like you, my friend, Hawk. They do not like what you do. In your aeroplane. I think they might want to cut off your hands and your feet, too, maybe." Simon looked up at the sky. "But I do not believe you killed their chickens."

I noticed commotion at the far end of the crowd.

"Thank you," I said softly.

Simon put his hands on the pistols at his sides and laughed loudly. "Now, about those hands and feet…"

From behind a line of men, Ella pushed through, followed by the man Simon sent off after her. "Hey—"

She was dressed in green fatigues. Her hair was tucked up under a bush hat. She carried a shotgun over her shoulder. Then she saw me.

"They would like to cut off his hands and his feet," Simon informed her.

She looked at Simon.

He smiled broadly and gestured to the village chief.

"Laisse le partir. Maintenant," she ordered. *"Maintenant."*

The man argued back vehemently, now in French.

Ella looked at Simon. *"A poulet?"*

"Eh, the Hawkman says no." Simon nodded my way.

Ella stepped over into the man's face. *"Non. Laisse le partir."*

The chief looked around at his tribe.

"Maintenant."

The chief looked threateningly down at Ella and bared his pointy teeth.

Moments later, a white hand gripped the chief's shoulder.

"I was in the neighborhood…" Roscoe said, sliding up beside the chief. "How is everybody doing?"

Far in the background, I could hear gasoline engines approaching.

"Dr. Mickleson…so good to see you again." He smiled at her, then noticed her gun. "Simon."

A serious look came over Simon's face.

"Alfalfa," I said.

"You look like hell."

"I've felt better."

"Mmm…I can imagine." Roscoe looked at the chief. He smiled.

Moments later, a 52 Commando Ferret armored car and two Jeeps pulled up and spread out behind the crowd, their machine guns manned by mercenaries. Sergeant Jack and his troops got out of the Jeeps armed with their rifles.

"Roscoe…You doing okay?" Jack asked.

"I invited some friends." Roscoe looked around the crowd. He then stared at Simon. "Now, did I hear somebody say something about chickens?"

Simon nodded, his big toothy smile coming back over his face again. He pointed at the chief. "They have lost their chickens. And they are blaming this man, here." Simon pointed at me.

"Chickens?" Roscoe looked down at the ground and slowly shook his head. He looked back at Simon. "Let's talk. You and me."

Simon nodded and they stepped off, far enough away that we could not hear them speak. Roscoe looked back and pointed at Ella.

She looked at me.

I shrugged.

Alfalfa nodded, then dug into his pocket and pulled out a wad of money. He counted out several bills and handed them to Simon. They spoke again, and Roscoe counted out even more bills, which went into Simon's pocket.

Simon came back and walked the chief away from me.

Roscoe strolled up to us and nodded to the men holding me. They backed off, and he pulled out a switchblade and cut the ropes on my arms.

"You know, you are not a cheap date," Roscoe said. "Good thing Ella and I showed up. You were looking a little lonely in this crowd."

Ella scowled.

We all watched as the chief wandered off with his money. The villagers quickly began to follow him.

Simon and Jack came over.

"I see you came dressed for the occasion," Roscoe said to Ella.

"What?" I asked.

Ella looked at Roscoe, then at me. "Father Bob. The Simbas took him on the road last night."

Alfalfa sighed. "Looks like our work here is not done yet."

~~~

The Trail

Ella, Roscoe, Jack, and Simon stood over the hood of Alfalfa's Jeep pouring over a map of the area. They took turns pointing at different spots. Jack and Simon argued. Roscoe and Ella listened.

I hung back, stretching the cramps out of my arms. I looked down towards the village, at the men who had taken me. Some stared back hard—as if I really had killed their chickens, I guess. They might well have cut off my hands and feet. No doubt. Then worse. Others swarmed the chief as he counted Roscoe's cash.

Ella wandered back to where I stood. "You okay?"

I nodded, staring down the tribesmen.

She looked back, too, then pulled me into the hut where I was held in. She set her shotgun by the door and stood in front of me. "Stand here."

"What?"

"Let me see." She turned my head her way and looked clinically into my eyes. "Follow my finger."

She held my chin and slowly moved her finger back and forth, then up and down in front of my face. She took my head in her hands and felt my skull, stopping halfway down along the back. "That's a nasty bump. You got a headache?"

"Not much anymore." I grimaced a bit.

She felt along my arms, testing my reactions at my elbows and wrists. "Grip my hands, hard. Okay. Pull my hands toward you.

Now, push them back."

"I'm fine."

"Hey. Who's the doctor here?" she asked.

"You are."

"Right. Now take off your clothes."

"What?"

"Come on." She started unbuttoning.

"But—" I grabbed her hands.

"Do it. Now."

"Okay. Okay." I opened up my flight suit.

Ella felt inside my flight suit around my neck and shoulders. Pushing up my t-shirt, she pressed around my stomach, then stooped down to check my legs. "Yeah. Just as I thought." She went over to the hut door and called out to Simon.

He came over.

She pointed at my legs.

I looked down and noticed the leeches.

Simon pulled out a cigarette, lit it, then handed it to Ella.

"You don't need to watch this," she told Simon, and he left. She came back to me and knelt down. "You have to burn them off. If you don't, the heads will stay attached and get infected. Now step out of your suit."

I did so reluctantly. I closed my eyes as she burned them off of me.

"That should do it," Ella said.

I opened my eyes. Alfalfa stood in the doorway of the hut.

"Well, well, well…What's going on in here?" he asked.

"If he keeps out of trouble, he might live another couple…of decades." Ella said, standing up and stepping back.

"Too bad." Roscoe tossed me a pair of blue jeans and a fresh shirt. "Put these on."

"Blue jeans?"

"They'll help with the leeches and the mosquitoes."

"Oh, good." As I dressed, I asked, "What happened to Father Bob?"

"They came through the mission yesterday, while I was in the village seeing patients." Ella went back to the door and shouldered her shotgun.

"Just him?"

Ella nodded.

"What about the gun thing?" I pointed at the shotgun over her shoulder. "I thought you didn't want them around."

She shrugged. "I hunted with my dad."

"Well, we're not shooting grouse," Roscoe said. He stared at Ella. "Just so you know how things are going to go. If we find the Simbas, we're going have to kill them."

"I'm going." She gave Alfalfa a hard look.

"Okay. I've got no problem with that." He looked at me. "You?"

I shook my head.

"Anyway, you'll be safer with us, I figure."

"Where are they taking him?" Ella asked.

"Stanleyville, I figure. They've been collecting hostages—for now anyway. But we need to get him back before they get him there."

Ella nodded.

"What about you?" Roscoe asked me. "You up for a ride in the country?"

"Yeah. I could use some fresh air," I answered.

"And what about him?" Roscoe nodded back towards Simon.

"He's good," Ella answered.

"Well, my friend Jack doesn't like him much," Roscoe said.

"He'll be okay."

After I was dressed, we walked back to the Jeeps.

"We'll put them behind the Ferret. Then, Jack. That way, he can keep an eye on them." Alfalfa smiled broadly. He called out, "Simon."

Ella and I looked over at him.

"Yes?"

"I think my friend, Hawk, here, would like his pistol back."

Jack reached out his hand towards Simon.

Simon smiled broadly. "Of course. Of course. I was just keeping it safe for him."

One of Simon's men handed him my holster. Simon looked at the gun fondly, then passed it to Jack, who brought it over to Roscoe.

Alfalfa pulled the pistol out of the holster. He smiled. "This looks government-issue."

"I've had it a while," I said. "Since the war."

Roscoe slid the pistol back into its holster and handed me the Colt. "I ought to report you…but I'll let it slide—*this time.*"

"Thanks."

He turned to Jack. "Let's mount up.'

The men started moving towards their vehicles.

"And keep an eye on him," Roscoe told Jack softly, pointing at Simon.

"You got it."

✳✳✳~~~✳✳✳

Jungleland

The Ferret took off first, followed by a Toyota truck filled with Simon's men in the back bed. Jack followed in his Jeep. Then Ella rode with Simon and two men in her Range Rover. Alfalfa and I brought up the rear in the other Jeep.

"Angel will be glad you're okay," Roscoe said

"Thanks for coming."

"All part of the job, don't you know. We are a full-service Agency. Besides, I was just twiddling my thumbs in Kamina when I found out."

"And Father Bob?"

"Hmmm…I think he may be okay for now. They want him north. But we got to get him and get him quick. I don't want them getting him to Stanleyville. That's going to get real ugly real soon."

I nodded.

The road narrowed, and the jungle swallowed us up. Roscoe drifted back a bit to avoid the red clay chunks off of the Land Rover.

"Anyway, you, sir, are one damned lucky guy," Alfalfa said. "First, you get your ass shot the hell out of the sky. I talked to Angel, and he said that was a serious stall-spin-crash-burn-cartwheeling wreck-and-a-half. Big, big flames. Aka-foosh."

I winced.

"Then, you land in the jungle without a damned scratch on you. When I got the call from Eric, I figured you'd head to the river. And then when I get to the village, there you are making time with Dr. Mickleson."

"But how did you know to find me in that village?"

Alfalfa smiled my way. "Simon's guys aren't the only ones who understand the native drumming."

I cleared my throat. "Would they have cut off my hands and feet?"

Roscoe shook his head. "Son, you don't want to know what they can do. They're not the Germans. No Stalags here in the jungle."

I looked forward and nodded my head.

"Which is why we have to get Father Bob. Pronto."

I looked at Alfalfa. He stared at the back of Jack's Jeep. No smile on his face. "So…Jack…and Simon?"

Roscoe snickered. "It's like being courtside at the Coliseum. Throw them all in, get some Cracker Jack, and let them sort it out. Jack's on our side, but I definitely would not get between his muzzle and any Simbas."

"And Simon?"

"Well, between Father Bob and Langely's slush funds, he's on our side—for now. Besides, he ain't stupid. When the government is finally done with Mad Mike and his Commandos and boot their sorry asses out of Congo, he'll have to get along with whoever is left."

"Who's that going to be?"

"Your guess is as good as mine. I'd put my money on Mobuto, myself."

"Who's he?"

"Right now? The guy with the most guns. He's in charge of the Congolese Army—such as it is."

I shook my head. "Way above my pay grade."

"I don't pick them—much. What with the Belgians, Commandos Five and Six, I think it will be the end of the Simbas, anyway."

"And what about Ella?"

Jungleland

"I don't like it, but I'd rather she be here. With you and me."

I nodded. I looked at my hands, thankful I still had them. The jungle became a blur of green as we drove.

Jeunesse

The exhaustion finally caught up with me, and I slept—not that Alfalfa made the ride comfortable. I was just that tired. I don't know how long I was out. Then shots rang out and woke me.

I looked up. Ella and Simon were pulled off to the right side of the road twenty yards in front of us halfway up the hill. Simon stood with his pistol drawn behind the Range Rover, talking to a man with an AK-47. Another armed man stood at the driver's door, blocking it to keep Ella inside.

The road curved up to the left, then slightly back down again. Jack jumped out of his Jeep and disappeared over the top. Roscoe sat behind the driver's wheel and watched.

Shaking off the sleep, I reached for the FN FAL at my side.

The Ferret's Browning fired into the bush.

Over the hill, Jack's machine gunner laced the low canopy to the left side of the road, shredding the greenery like confetti. Another Commando fired his rifle from behind the engine compartment. His driver aimed and shot from behind the rear quarter panel. Simon's men fired from behind the Toyota and the Ferret.

I jumped out and searched the treeline. I didn't see anything to shoot at.

Our machine gunner fed short bursts into the jungle.

Alfalfa sat in his seat and shook his head.

The firing stopped. Everyone stared into the trees.

An AK-47 lit off a magazine out of the bush against the Ferret.

Everyone's guns focused on that spot and let loose.

Then it was quiet again.

Roscoe grabbed his M14 and got out. He hugged the treeline and moved forward up next to Jack. He pushed and shoved Jack and Simon's guys to spread them out on both sides of the road using the vehicles, trees, and rocks for cover.

Ella pushed her way out of the Range Rover and came up beside me at the Jeep with her shotgun across her chest.

"What are you shooting at?" she asked me.

"Nothing yet. I don't see anyone." In the sky, you don't shoot unless you have a shot. I saw nothing.

A couple of bullets pinged off the Ferret. Automatic fire cut a stitch between the Toyota and Jack's Jeep.

Simon's guys sprayed the jungle.

"Maintenez votre feu," Roscoe called out. *"Maintenez votre feu!"*

The return fire slowly sputtered out.

Suddenly, the heat and humidity of the jungle pressed down on me. Of course, the jungle was quiet.

I looked at Ella and shrugged my shoulders.

We crouched down and leaned against our Jeep.

Roscoe moved up to the Ferret and spread out Simon's guys.

Occasional rounds rang out from the treeline.

Jack came back our way. He squatted down at our side and gave Ella a long look. "You guys okay?"

We both nodded.

"That thing loaded?" he asked Ella.

"Yes."

"Good." He waved Simon over our way.

"Yes, Jack."

"Take two of your guys and set up a line in the back here."

"Are they behind us, too?" Simon asked.

"Not sure." He stared at Simon. "Just do it."

Simon stared back.

Occasional rounds scattered among the group.

Satisfied with the defensive lines up front, Alfalfa came back our way. He asked Simon, "What do you think?"

"They are all *fou*—just *dingue,* man."

"We all go a little crazy now, don't we." Roscoe smiled. "Get down there at the bend and set up a perimeter."

Simon nodded. "Okay…okay."

Roscoe watched them move away. "Next week, we'll get organized."

"You smell it?" Jack asked.

"Yeah. Up front," Roscoe answered. He looked at me and Ella. *"Dagga*…marijuana. They'll be coming soon."

Ella frowned.

"Puts them in the mood, I guess.," Jack said.

"Get with your guys," Alfalfa said. "I'll go up with the rest of Simon's boys up front."

"And us?" Ella asked.

"Don't shoot until you see the whites of their eyes." Roscoe winked and took off towards the front of the column to check his perimeter.

Jack looked at Ella with the shotgun. He started to say something but shook his head. "Be careful back here.…and watch those guys."

He pointed towards Simon. Then Jack rejoined his men.

We sat with our backs against the side of Roscoe's Jeep.

Ella held her shotgun between her legs and rested her forehead on the barrel. "Have you ever shot anyone?"

My FN FAL lay across my lap. "I've shotdown airplanes. I've shot at men on the ground. I know I've killed my share, but…"

"It's different, right?"

I nodded. I looked at Ella.

"Clay pigeons and ducks," she said. "And, really, not that many."

"What are we doing here?"

She looked at Simon down the road, then up at Jack. "I—I just don't know anymore."

"Father Bob, right?"

She leaned back against the Jeep. She shook her head. "I just wanted to help somehow."

An occasional shot pinged off the Ferret and the Jeeps.

"Well, now we're in a hell of a pickle," I said. I checked around the front bumper. A rip of automatic fire cut up between our Jeep and the Range Rover. "Yup. They're definitely still out there."

"Don't do that."

"Right."

"What will they do to him?"

"The Simbas? Bad stuff—I don't know. I've never seen it, but…it's bad. Roscoe's seen it. He's seen a lot. And it's bad. Evil bad."

"So, we have to get him back."

I nodded.

"Okay, then." She nodded. "But… who are they?"

"*Jeunesse.*"

"Kids?"

"With machine guns and sharpened bicycle chains. And machetes, too"

"Kids."

"I won't be buying them off with licorice."

Ella pressed her head against the shotgun. "Why?"

It happened suddenly. The jungle erupted with small arms fire, ricocheting off the vehicles and dirt.

Just beyond Simon and his men, twenty or thirty Simbas charged out of the jungle, heading our way, firing their AK-47s wildly like fire hoses. Most of the shots went over our heads.

Simon and his men returned fire. Roscoe's machine gunner turned and began spitting out brass onto our heads.

I came around Ella and, without thinking, took aim and pulled the trigger. A man fell. I aimed again and again.

Our fire shredded the on-rush of men.

"Hawk—" Ella called out.

She moved around me and fired two quick blasts towards our side of the road. One man fell.

Simbas had crossed the road and were moving our way along the trees.

I patted the machine gunner's leg and pointed. He turned his muzzle their way and fired. The air filled with the green confetti of leaves overhead.

I pushed Ella back and rapidly fired a new magazine. Not even aiming. Just shooting. Twenty shots. I put in another magazine, pulling the trigger again and again and again in semi-automatic mode.

Then it was over. As quickly as it started. There was no one left standing to shoot.

Simbas littered the road behind us. Simon and his men were

up moving quickly through the bodies, firing occasionally at wounded men on the ground.

Upfront Jack's guys were up and firing down into the treeline. Their rate of fire fell off.

"You okay?" I asked, putting another magazine in my rifle.

Ella sat on the ground behind me, asking herself, "What am I doing here? What am I doing here?"

Simon

"Clear!" They shouted out ahead.

"Clear!"

"Clear!"

The callouts came from all around us.

I sat down next to Ella.

"And now I am a part of it all," she said. "Of this war."

"You didn't ask for this."

"No. No, I didn't. Not for this."

"Nobody does." I grabbed her shoulder with my arm and squeezed gently.

We sat quietly for a little while, then stood. Behind us was a tangled mess of bodies spread out along the road. Some were dressed in khakis. Some like natives. Simon's men casually went from man to man, digging through their pockets. There seemed to be little to take, except for unused magazines for their AK-47s.

One of Simon's men noticed us. He looked back at Ella and me. He smiled and waved his hand.

Ella gave him a scornful look.

His smile melted. He shrugged his shoulders and went back to searching the dead bodies.

Ella started towards the dead Simbas.

I followed as she walked among them. "You were right. Some

of them are just children. They're just kids. Like the ones in the village."

"Kids who were going to kill us." I gently took her arm. "Come on, let's go upfront."

I led her away from the bodies.

Three of Jack's men were gathered by the Ferret. They spoke loudly, pointing into the jungle.

Jack stood out in front of the armored car, looking down the hill.

When the men saw us coming, they quieted down.

Jack heard. He moved our way and met us when we got to the men.

"No harm. No foul," he said, smiling.

There were not as many dead bodies up front.

Jack eyeballed Ella as she looked around. "Most of them are still in the brush."

"Everybody okay up here?" I asked.

"They don't shoot so well. My men are okay. A couple of Simon's guys got scratched up a bit." He looked at Ella. "You want to take a look?"

Ella was looking down the hill. "What's that?"

Roscoe and Simon were talking to three Simba rebels standing in a line, surrounded by Simon's men, aiming their rifles at them. One of the men fell over and was forced back to his feet by one of the guards.

"Is he hurt?" Ella asked.

"We'll see what they know," Jack said.

Roscoe spoke to the man on the far left. Simon translated. One of Simon's guys slammed his rifle butt into the man's stomach. He collapsed but was brought to his feet again quickly, gasping for breath.

"Hey—" Ella moved forward.

Jack grabbed her arm. "You don't want to go down there."

While the first man collected himself, Roscoe and Simon moved on to the middle man.

Ella pulled her arm from Jack's hand.

"We will see what they know," Jack said again slowly.

"Ella," I said. "If they know where Father Bob is…"

The second man appeared to be more talkative.

"That man is injured," Ella said. "He's bleeding."

Jack looked down at them. He shrugged. "It happens. It's war."

Jack and Ella stared at one another.

"Why don't you take a look at Simon's men and help them out?"

Roscoe started walking back our way. As he approached, he said, "They are up ahead of us. Twenty or thirty clicks."

A shot rang out from down the hill. The first Simba fell back and collapsed.

Simon moved down the line and quickly shot the other two men in their heads with his pistol. He holstered it and began to walk back up the hill.

"Hey!" Ella called out and began to move his way.

Jack grabbed Ella's arm. "You really don't need to go down there. There's nothing you can do for them now."

They stared each other down.

Ella pulled her arm away and met Simon by the Ferret. "You shot them."

Simon put his hands on his hips and looked down at Ella.

I took a step forward.

"Hawk." Roscoe shouldered his M14 and put his hands into

his pants pockets. He shook his head slightly.

We watched.

A half-smile came over Simon's face looking down into Ella's eyes. "Yes. Yes, I did."

"They were unarmed," Ella said, taking a step closer to Simon.

Simon looked at us. He looked over at Jack's men off to the side.

"Well, I guess, maybe, they are on our side," Jack said. "For now…"

Down the hill, Simon's men began searching the bodies.

"You killed them," Ella said.

Simon looked up at the sky. He took a deep breath. He smiled broadly showing his teeth and looked back down at Ella. "Yes. I did kill them."

"But—"

"Doctor…look around." He spread his arms out to the jungle. "Where are the policemen? We have no lawyers here. We have no judges. And they have your friend."

Ella bit her lower lip.

Simon stepped closer. His smile fell away. He spoke a little more softly, though we could still hear. "Do you know what they will do to Father Bob? I do. I know. I have seen it many, many times." He shook his head slowly.

Ella looked away.

"I do not want to tell you about it," Simon whispered. "You do not want to know."

"We need to move out," Roscoe said. He turned to me. "Maybe you should ride with Ella."

I nodded.

Alfalfa headed towards his Jeep. "Come on."

"We need to find him…quickly now." Simon smiled broadly again. "And that is why he pays me."

Ella looked into Simon's eyes.

He nodded, then stepped around her and followed Roscoe up the hill.

Jack motioned to his guys to load up.

Ella looked off into the jungle.

"Come on," I said. "We need to go."

"Are we just going to leave them all here like this?" she turned to ask.

Roscoe and Simon stopped to look back at her.

"We really do need to get moving," Alfalfa said. "They won't wait."

He and Simon got into his Jeep.

Ella sighed, and we walked to the Land Rover.

I got behind the wheel. We started our engines, and I pulled behind Jack, followed by Roscoe and Simon.

Ella stared at the three bodies as we drove by.

~~~

The Churchyard

It was a long, very quiet drive. I tried again and again to talk to her, but all Ella wanted was to look out at the passing green scenery. So, I gave up and practiced my formation flying, trying to keep a consistent twenty-five yards off of Jack's rear bumper.

The sun was getting low when we pulled out into a clearing with a worn-down stone church and several small abandoned houses.

Sergeant Jack's men jumped out and quickly began searching the buildings.

Ella slid out of the front door and walked off the opposite way.

I stood by Range Rover. Alfalfa came up beside me.

"Don't go far," Roscoe called out after Ella.

She stopped for a moment without looking back, then wandered to the edge of the jungle, staring into it.

Alfalfa shrugged at me. "We'll put up here for the night."

"How far are the Simbas?" I asked.

"I can't imagine they are making good time with hostages in tow. We'll catch them tomorrow, I'm sure." Roscoe looked at me. "How is she doing?"

"It ain't exactly been living the Peace Corps dream for her."

Roscoe shrugged. "Not much of a war…"

"But it's the only one we've got," I answered.

"Eh." He looked at Ella, then back at me. "Not much we can do about that now. She's in for the long haul. Can't exactly leave her all alone in the middle of the jungle."

I nodded.

"Did she shoot that thing?" Roscoe pointed at her shotgun on the back seat of the Range Rover.

"Yeah. Yeah, she did, actually. Saved my butt, too."

"Hmm…Anyway, keep an eye on her. We don't need to be tracking down any more hostages." Roscoe leaned into me and whispered, "You can do that, right? I mean, you don't mind, do you? Keeping an eye on her, that is."

"No. I don't mind."

"Good. You're a real sport." Alfalfa went over to the church to talk with Jack.

I leaned against the Range Rover watching the activity in the churchyard.

Jack's men reappeared from the empty houses, guns lowered. Relaxed, they lit up cigarettes and began joking around.

Simon's men scattered out to collect plantains and pineapples.

I watched Ella pace at the edge of the jungle. This war wasn't what she wanted. It wasn't exactly what I signed up for, chasing rebels on the ground. But it was Father Bob.

Suddenly, it was dark. No sunset, just night. It was the equator.

I wandered over to bring Ella back to the church for dinner. I just stood ten feet back. She was wandering among the rows of a small cemetery.

She turned, saw me, then continued pacing back past me again. She shook her head as she went by.

I watched her pace off fifteen or twenty feet to the end of the row, then step around and come back again past the next line of graves. She stopped in front of me. "Are they out there? The Simbas?"

"Probably."

"How could he?"

"Simon?" I asked.

"How could he just shoot them?"

"Honestly, if he didn't, Jack's guys would have done it. I'm sure."

"Barbarians." She turned and looked out at the jungle.

We were standing at the unwoven edges of civilization, a ruined church behind us. Men with murder, mayhem, and worse in mind hiding out in the jungle…and behind us, as well.

She turned and asked, "It doesn't bother you, does it?"

"What?"

She spread her arms out. "Death."

I thought. "Mine does. And yours…and Father Bob's."

"And Simon?"

"Not so much, I suppose."

"Yeah. Me neither." She shook her head. "I suppose it should, though. I—I just can't…"

"He's working for Father Bob. At least for now."

"Yeah…yeah, I know. I know."

"His world…" I shrugged. "I guess they play by very different rules. This isn't Washington DC."

"Rules that let you shoot people in the head."

I could feel a grimace latch onto my face. "It's not one big happy family of man out here—or anywhere. Never has been."

Ella looked at me.

"A whetstone for a man's character," I said. "And a graveyard for illusions."

"And Jack?"

"He knows what he's doing. Him and his guys. It's what they signed up for to get their checks from Mad Mike."

She stepped between the graves to come by me. "What about you?"

"I signed up to fly airplanes."

"And kill people that way."

"I don't hate them."

"What's the difference?"

I looked down and kicked a clod of clay at a headstone. "I never asked, you know. No one did."

"Asked for what?"

"It was like a tidal wave. You couldn't swim against it. No one did. You're twenty-two, strapping yourself into a P-51. All by yourself, you know. All by yourself…"

"You came back."

"Of course, I did. I just don't know how, when I think about it all again, but I did."

"A double ace, right?"

"It's not the numbers…"

"And since?"

"God help me, I missed it."

"The killing?"

"The flying…the flying. Alaska was raw. On the edge." I looked out at the jungle trees. "But nobody was trying to shoot me down."

"Which they did, right?"

I nodded. "Anyway, what does it matter?"

"These were just kids, some of them. Little kids."

"I didn't know, really."

Jungleland

Ella turned away. "I killed them…I shot those boys back there."

I turned her back my way. I gently raised her face by her chin. "They were killers."

Ella pulled away. She stepped towards the church.

"They were going to kill you. They were going to kill me."

She stopped and looked back at me.

"Did I say thank you?"

She shook her head.

I went over beside her. "Thank you."

"And tomorrow?"

I sighed. "Come on. Let's get back."

"You're welcome, I guess."

"Come on…"

I put my arm around her shoulders, and we walked back.

~~~

We took our plates back to the Range Rover, leaned on the front hood, and ate in silence. Jack's guys sat in a circle in the shadows of the Ferret. Simon's guys collected on the other side of the churchyard. Roscoe picked up his plate and came over.

He took a big bite of pineapple. He looked over his shoulder. "You trust any of these guys?"

I shrugged my shoulders. "For what?"

Alfalfa looked towards Ella.

I looked at her.

"I'll sleep with my shotgun," she said. "I've used it once already today."

"There you go." Roscoe smiled. "But still…"

"We'll take one of the houses," I said.

"I don't need—" Ella said.

"We will take one of the houses." I stared her down.

"Yeah. That might be best. I'll bunk with Jack's guys in the church. That'll be cozy."

"And Simon?" I asked.

"Half of them are asleep already, scattered around the courtyard," Roscoe said. He looked at Ella. "Sorry to drag you into this."

"I came with Simon. I suppose I should have known what might happen,"

Alfalfa nodded. "Okay. Get some rest. We'll be busy tomorrow."

He went back over with Jack's guys.

I grabbed blankets out of the back of the Range Rover.

Ella followed me into the stone house. We set up our beds against opposite walls.

"There will be more of them tomorrow," Ella said.

"I think so."

"There will be more killing, won't there."

I nodded.

She lay down and closed her eyes. Soon she was snoring softly.

I spent the night watching over her.

~~~

The Plantation

It seemed like I only got an hour's sleep or so. I let Ella drive the Range Rover at first light, following Jack's Jeep with Alfalfa and Simon behind us. It wasn't long before I nodded off in the passenger seat, even as rough as the road was.

The sun was high in the sky when we pulled off to the side near the top of a hill. Ella's door closing woke me. She went up ahead of me, following Alfalfa and Simon to join Sergeant Jack at the back of the Ferret. Jack and Simon's guys got out and milled around. I sat, trying to shake the cobwebs from my head.

Roscoe and Jack moved towards the top of the hill enough to see over.

Ella stood back away from Simon. He turned to look at her. He smiled.

I shut my eyes. When I looked again, they were speaking calmly so it seemed.

I got out and headed their way.

"Mr. Hawk," Simon said as I approached.

I looked at Ella.

She shrugged.

"What's going on?" I asked.

"It seems like we may have found them," Ella said.

"Where?"

"There is a plantation down in the next valley," Simon said.

I nodded, then headed up to Roscoe and Jack.

They scanned the far horizon with their binoculars.

"What gives?" I asked.

"Looks like a good old-fashion Boy Scout Jamboree down there," Alfalfa said.

"How many do you think?" asked Jack.

"I figure thirty…maybe forty," Roscoe said.

"Any sign of Father Bob?" I asked.

"They seem to have a small group they've herded into a shelter down there. I haven't seen him, though."

"You think these are the right guys?" Jack asked.

"I'd say probably yes." He handed me the binoculars.

I looked between the banana trees at the group of buildings. "Where's that shelter?"

"Down to the right. They're all inside now."

"So, what do we do?" Jack asked.

"I don't know if they're expecting us or just waiting for another group or maybe just stocking up for the last push up north…"

"Well, we shouldn't make them wait long," Jack said.

"Yeah…yeah…What do you think?"

"You see any guards or a perimeter?"

"No," I said.

"Good," said Jack.

Alfalfa pulled a map out of his back pocket and held it up. "Look familiar?"

I shook my head.

"A little bird-dogging, don't you know."

Roscoe led us back to Jack's Jeep and laid the map out on the hood. He waved Simon over to us. Ella followed.

Jungleland

We all stared at the map.

"We should come in from the east," Jack finally said.

Roscoe nodded. "Yeah, we can move off on this side road down here, curl around the back of this grove of trees, then move up along this line here and come at them from the backside. We should be able to spread out among the rows and move quickly through the tree lines."

"All of us?" Jack asked.

"Simon, can you move your guys into this area here?" Roscoe asked, pointing to a wooded area on the west side of the plantation buildings. "There's plenty of cover moving down that way against the side of the ridge here."

"There is no road there," Simon said.

"Yeah, you'll have to move through the jungle. It's maybe four or five klicks."

"And?" Simon asked.

"I want you guys to move into these areas, here and here." Roscoe pointed at positions a bit southwest of the buildings. "Spread your teams out enough to cause confusion, right? Try to get within two hundred fifty yards and dig in. We'll want you to provide cover for us coming in from the back end."

"How many are there?" Simon asked.

Alfalfa looked at Jack. "Eh, probably twenty or so. Not so bad, really. We can take them easy."

"Yes. Okay," said Simon. "Yes, we can do this."

"Can you hit anything with those AKs?" Jack asked.

Simon gave Jack a hard look. "My men are good."

"Listen to me," Roscoe said. "No automatic fire. We need every shot to count. Do you understand? I don't want any fire hosing."

Simon looked from Jack to Roscoe. "Yes. I understand."

"And make sure they walk their fire up to the Simba positions. Do you understand?" Roscoe said. "If you shoot high and miss, it's dead lead. But a ricochet can kill them, too."

"Yes. We will see to it," Simon said.

"Good. We're high enough here to get through to arrange some air support." Roscoe pointed to the Ferret. "Get Eric for me."

Jack grinned. "That will definitely help."

"Can you get in position in two hours?" Roscoe asked Simon.

Simon nodded.

Roscoe scratched his head, figuring. "We'll have them on station by five at the latest. That gives you three hours. We'll drive your truck around with us. Okay? Get your guys moving down through the first canopy. Stay out of sight, damn it. We'll go when the Makasi hit the plantation."

Simon hesitated.

"We'll have the truck down there for you guys. You can't drive it down that way."

Simon nodded.

"Good luck. We'll meet up down there," Roscoe said. "But stay put in your positions until we clear the area. No friendly fire. Understand? Don't move in until we tell you."

Simon turned and marched back to his guys.

"Roscoe, Eric is up," Jack said.

Alfalfa grabbed up the map and headed to the Ferret to talk to Eric on the radio.

Jack stepped up beside me. "I don't know if I trust them. Do you?"

"They did alright at the ambush," I said.

"Kill or be killed. Backs against the wall, then." Jack said.

Simon's men collected their guns, their ammo, and slowly trailed off into the bush.

Roscoe came back and watched with us.

"You trust those guys?" Jack asked.

"I guess it depends upon how much Father Bob promised to pay them, huh," Roscoe said.

"We'll see what we see, that's for sure," Jack said.

The last of Simon's men got swallowed up by the low canopy.

"We'll have the T-6s overhead at five," Roscoe said. "Put a guy in the back of Simon's pickup. Let's get ready to rollout."

"Let's go make some noise," said Jack. He headed off for his guys.

"What about us?" Ella asked.

Roscoe laid the map back out on the hood of the Jeep. "We are going to drive down into the back forty of this plantation on this side road here. I saw them taking hostages into this building…here."

"Father Bob?"

"I think so. Looks like a couple of other folks as well. So, you and Hawk are going to follow behind our line, and after we move through these buildings, you will need to get them out of there and into the Range Rover and pull them back out."

Ella looked at the map. "Will this work?"

Roscoe smiled. "No problem."

She looked at me.

"Yeah. No problem." I smiled but did not sound convincing.

Roscoe gathered up his map. "Just stick with Hawk. He'll take care of you."

"I guess you're with me," I said.

"Great." Ella gave me a nervous smile.

~~~

I got behind the wheel of the Range Rover, pulled behind Jack's Jeep and headed down the hill to the east. It took an hour and fifteen minutes to wind our way down the back road to the east side of the plantation trees. Roscoe spread us out and had me park twenty-five yards back behind the Ferret.

Alfalfa stopped by the Range Rover and stuck his head inside Ella's door on the passenger side. "How are we doing? Okay?"

"So, is this going to work?" Ella asked him again.

He smiled. "I give us a sixty—maybe seventy percent chance."

"That doesn't sound very encouraging," she said.

"I don't know. What do you think, Hawk?"

"Of working, right?" I said.

"Yeah…I think so." Roscoe looked at Ella and smiled. "So, Doc, do you give one hundred percent guarantees on all of your work?"

Ella just looked at Alfalfa.

"I think seventy percent is pretty darn good, actually," he said to me. "Sorry. No guarantees. No warranties."

"We'll be fine," I said. "Just fine."

"The boys should be overhead in twenty minutes or so. We'll let them cut things up, then we'll move in. You stay back behind the Ferret by fifty yards, at least. Once we push the Simbas back from the group of buildings, you and Ella go in and get Father Bob. Got it?"

"Got it," I said.

"Then get the hell out of there. Leave the fighting to Jack and

Simon's guys. Just get him back to the hilltop. ASAP."

I nodded. "Got it."

He looked at Ella. "We'll be fine. Seventy percent are good odds for us."

Ella watched Alfalfa walk up to the Ferret and get on the radio.

Ella looked at me and asked again, "So, is this going to work?"

I wanted to tell her the old Moltke saying that "no plan survives contact with the enemy," but said instead, "It will work."

Ella looked off through her window at Jack's men in the Jeep racking their weapons.

"Where are your shells? Did you reload?"

She looked at me, then grabbed a medical satchel off the back floor.

I took it and pushed three new shells into her shotgun.

"I don't want to do this," she said.

"We're not going to do any shooting. We'll go in, get Father Bob and get the hell out of here."

"But—"

"Just in case." I handed her the gun. "I'll go into the shelter. You just watch the door. Okay?"

She nodded.

"Jack's guys will have pushed the Simbas off. We'll be okay."

"I don't want to do this."

I grabbed my FN FAL. I dropped the magazine and opened the breech. "Yeah. Me neither, too."

I heard them far, far off. The Texans.

"What?" Ella asked.

"They're coming." I reloaded the magazine, locked a shell in the breech, then set the safety on. "Listen."

We couldn't see them from beneath the treetops, but their

engines grew from a murmur to a low growl to a roar.

Roscoe stood on the back of the Ferret directing traffic over the radio.

The aircraft engines filled the valley with noise. Roscoe wound his hand above his head to signal us to start our engines. He ran left to his Jeep.

"Ready?" I asked.

Ella shook her head and said, "Yes."

I turned the key.

I couldn't see them, but machine guns from the Texans cut a swath up the path to the buildings. Quickly, a second aircraft swept through launching rockets. It came upon us quickly.

Small arms fire rose back up into the sky from the Simbas.

A lull in the fighting, then the first plane came back through, launching rockets, then machine guns.

I was hoping Simon's men had opened fire from the other side.

I couldn't see Roscoe give the signal, but the Ferret began moving forward, slowly. Then, he picked up speed.

I put the Range Rover into gear, let him move ahead another twenty-five yards, then we headed towards the plantation buildings.

"I don't want to do this," Ella said.

"I know."

~~~

The Simbas

Fifty yards back, I couldn't see forward from the dust kicked up by the Ferret. But again, I did not want to be an open target, so I followed the storm. To the left and right, Jeeps sped along in line with the Ferret.

As we reached the end of the plantation, the mounted Jeep machine guns opened up, firing ahead.

The Ferret stopped at the first of the shacks. It's turret twisted, spitting out tracers from its Browning M1919.

I slowed, then stopped quickly.

Enemy soldiers fired back from the sides of the buildings.

The Ferret's machine gun cut into the stone wall and drove them back.

Jack's Jeep turned and caught them from behind. They retreated quickly. Then Jack pushed on.

I couldn't see through the compound to whether Simon's men were engaged.

The Ferret moved forward slowly. He raked down the aisle between the buildings, right then quickly pivoted left and fired.

I stayed parked. I could see the building up ahead, but the area had not been cleared yet.

Ella gripped and re-gripped her shotgun, staring straight ahead.

Maybe it was safe, but sitting back alone just waiting was hell. Most of the tracers coming our way went overhead. I couldn't help but duck a bit. It's different being on the ground. Just the noise was overwhelming.

Roscoe's Jeep disappeared off to the left.

Simon's pickup veered off to the right around Jack, the men in back firing their rifles over the side.

There was no shape to the battle from where we were parked. Overhead, it all seems so straight forward and simple. The Simbas are here. The Mercs are there. And they all go at it.

The Ferret moved slowly forward, abreast of our building.

I waited, watching.

Overhead the Texans made one last pass on the Simba positions.

Then the Ferret moved forward quickly.

In a moment, my foot came off the brake, and I sped forward, pushing Ella back into the seat.

I skittered around tree roots and pulled in front of the shelter where Roscoe saw the hostages taken.

I got out, and called to Ella, "You. Watch from here."

I ran up beside the front door. I took a deep breath and pounded hard at the door with the butt end of my rifle. I looked down and switched the safety to semi-auto.

Ella got out and ran to the corner of the building.

No shots came out of the building. I took a deep breath, slipped in, and slid in a low crouch to the left with my rifle ready to fire.

"Bob! Bob, are you in here?"

"Hawk?" A weak cry.

The building was twenty feet long. I scanned for Father Bob. "Where the hell are you?"

"Here. On the right. I think my leg is broken."

I slid down the wall. "Any Simbas?"

"No. No, just me and two women."

My eyes adjusted to the dim lighting. I saw him leaning back between stacks of fertilizer barrels.

I ran his way. "Can you walk?"

"A little."

"Which leg?"

"My right."

I went to lift him. "Come on, help him out."

One of the women took his arm over her shoulder on the left, and we quickly moved towards the front door.

We headed towards the passenger side rear door of the Range Rover.

"Father Bob," Ella said.

I pulled open the door and helped him in.

"Get in. Get in back," I said to the women.

Something behind her caught Ella's eye. She turned and looked to see a young Simba step out from behind the building, armed with a machete. She pointed her shotgun but did not fire.

He froze. The boy was only twelve or thirteen-years-old.

"Shoot him," I said, raising my rifle.

Ella hesitated.

A second rebel came out from behind the building with an AK-47. He fired a spray of automatic fire.

I pulled my trigger again and again.

I don't know where he came from, but Jack pulled up from the back and unloaded into the two Simbas until they fell.

"Hawk," Jack called out. He pointed.

Ella was coiled up on the ground in a fetal position. Blood soaked through her abdomen.

I ran over to her.

"I don't want to do this," she moaned. "I don't want to…"

~~~

The King Bee

I had not noticed that the main noise of shooting moved off and away towards Simon's men.

When Roscoe came back our way, I was over her body.

"Damnit," he said and pulled away to find the Ferret.

I rolled Ella gently on her back. "Lay still. Lay still."

I pulled the bottom of her shirt apart.

Jack brought me a medical kit. "How bad?"

"I don't know." I slowly pressed around the blotch of blood in the lower right side of her abdomen.

"That looks bad," Jack said.

"Yeah, yeah. I know." I asked Ella, "What do I do?"

She could only groan.

Roscoe came back. "I've got a chopper coming."

He pulled me out of the way and began digging into her wound.

Ella groaned.

"It's twenty minutes out," Alfalfa said. "Jack, bring your Jeep around. We've got to get her moved out to the clearing."

They lifted Ella and gently laid her on the hood. Roscoe drove. I walked beside, holding her hand and pressing on her wound to stop the bleeding.

"What about the old guy?" Jack said.

"His leg is broken," I said.

Jack went back and followed in the Range Rover.

Coming to the clearing, Simon's men were searching the bodies of the dead.

Simon paused to watch us pass by.

We stopped at the edge of the open area and waited for what seemed like hours.

Ella gripped my hand hard and squeezed. She moaned softly.

The rip of helicopter blades grew in the valley.

A King Bee swooped down and landed. We drove her up and gently laid her on the floor of the chopper.

Jack brought over Father Bob and loaded him on. The two women hostages stepped in.

"Go on. Get in," Alfalfa said to me. "Take care of her."

As I climbed aboard, a medic was already working on Ella's wounds.

I leaned back against the front bulkhead and watched.

Roscoe and Jack backed out of the rotor wash.

Butterflies clung to her to drink her blood.

The engine wound up, and we drifted up and away.

~~~

Sabena

"What are you going to do?"

"I don't know. I guess just go home."

"Home, where? Chicago? Los Angeles? Anchorage?"

"Hmmm…good question."

We sat drinking in a bar at the Leopoldville airport. A long, long way from the plantation and the war.

"Can you just desert like that?" Father Bob asked.

I smiled. "It's *Jungleland*. I don't have a contract."

Father Bob nodded and sipped his scotch.

"How's your leg?"

"It is now to the point of just being a pain in the ass. I just want the cast off already."

"And where are you going?"

"Well…I think I got the religion worked right out of me. It's, you know, hard to wrap your head around terrible things happening like that."

"Yeah. Like that."

Ella never made it back. She died on the helicopter. I closed my eyes and saw it again.

"I'm sorry," the medic said sadly. He leaned back away from her body. His hands covered with blood. "They hit an artery. There was nothing I could do. I'm sorry."

"I think I'll head back to Los Angeles."

Father Bob nodded.

"You want to come?"

"I don't know. Maybe…I've got no place else to be."

"Well, think about it."

The public address system announced that our Sabena flight would soon be boarding.

"That's us," Father Bob said.

We finished our drinks and headed to the gate.

Sparks was there searching for us. "About time, damn it. I want to get the hell out of here."

We stood in line and presented our tickets and boarding passes to the gate agent, then walked out into the heat on the tarmac and headed to the Boeing 707.

"Hawk." Alfalfa wandered out from around the front landing gear.

I stepped out of line.

"I couldn't let my favorite merc fly off without saying goodbye."

"I told you. I'm not a merc."

"Yeah, whatever." Roscoe shoved his hands in his pants pockets. "Where you headed?"

I shook my head. "You know this flight goes to Brussels."

"And then?"

"K Street."

"Her dad?"

I nodded.

"You know, I did not see it. It wasn't supposed to be that way. I tried. I really did."

"It was a kid," I said.

"She should have shot him. She should have shot them both dead."

"But it was a kid."

"Yeah, well, he's dead now, too."

"I—anyway, it's over."

Alfalfa looked off down the runway that would take us away. "No. Not really. It never is."

"Yeah, you're right."

"Hawk! They are waiting on you," Sparks called out from the bottom of the jet stair. "You damn sure don't want to miss your airplane."

"Tell them to wait a minute," Alfalfa called out. "And after K Street?"

"I think I'll head home to California."

Alfalfa nodded. "Good. Take some time. I don't get stateside much, but what the hell, you never know. Maybe I'll stop by for a drink."

We shook hands. "Yeah. Do that sometime."

"You've got to have a plan, right?"

I turned and headed towards the plane. When I looked back, Roscoe was gone already.

"Idiots," Sparks said. "Come on, let's go home,"

We got on the plane and left.

~~~

K Street

I met him at the Mayflower Hotel. He was tall and lanky with the hungry look of a lobbyist, dressed up pretty in a pinstriped three-piece suit, with a dark red tie. I stood up from the wing-back chair in the lobby.

”Mr. Byrd,” he said, reaching out his hand.

“Mr. Mickleson.”

He turned me toward the Rib Room restaurant and led me that way. We went directly to a table with only a nod to the *maitre 'd.* A waiter brought him a martini without asking.

“And for you, sir?” the waiter asked.

“Coffee, please. Black.”

Mr. Mickleson took a sip of gin. Then another. He set his glass down gently.

I looked at him. He started to ask something then stopped. I could see the look of him around her eyes. There was a hard set there. One that took her to Africa.

“Ella wrote that she met a pilot who flew in the war,” he said. “Then up in Alaska, too.”

I leaned back as the waiter set down my coffee.

“The usual, Mr. Mickleson?” he asked.

“Yes, please.” He said to me, “A small ribeye steak.”

I nodded. “Medium, please.”

“Yes, sir.” The waiter quickly left again.

"That would have been me," I finally answered.

"You flew Mustangs?"

I nodded. "Guilty as charged. I was in the 357th Fighter Group out of Yoxford. I flew in forty-four and forty-five."

"I served at the Pentagon. The Navy Bureau of Aeronautics." He took another sip of gin. "And there, in Africa?"

"I flew T-6s against the rebels."

"A mercenary."

"I was…let's say, on loan."

He nodded. "And your brother was a doctor?"

I took a long sip of coffee. "Yes. A plastic surgeon in Los Angeles."

"He was killed?"

"It's been a while."

He stared down into his nearly empty drink.

The waiter suddenly appeared with a second, set it quietly down, then left.

"I've talked to friends I have at the State Department."

"What did they tell you?"

"Nothing much really." He sighed. "Some kind of rebel action of some sort."

"Did you talk to the C.I.A.?"

"I don't know anyone there." He stared me down. "You know what happened, though, don't you."

I nodded.

"That's why you're here."

"A friend of ours was taken hostage by the rebels. Father Bob. He ran the mission in her village."

Mr. Mickleson leaned in to listen.

"It's a tough place, sir. The rebels are brutal. They all are."

"All?"

I thought about Simon. "It's a war zone."

He leaned back. He took a drink. "I—we did not want her to go."

"I know. But you weren't going to stop her."

"No…no, we weren't."

The waiter served our steaks. We began eating.

"How did you find out what happened?"

"I was there. With her."

"With her?"

I chewed a bite of steak. He didn't need to know all the details. "We tracked down the rebels at a banana plantation. It was a group of us. Some mercenaries. Some tribesmen."

"You and Ella?"

I nodded.

"And the C.I.A."

"We had some help that way."

"Who?"

I shook my head. "It doesn't really matter. Some guy…"

"Some guy?"

"I don't really know his name."

He knew I was lying.

"Ella and I, we found Father Bob. At the plantation." I hesitated. "It should have been okay. It should have been all right."

"But…"

"Some of the rebels are just kids."

"Kids?"

"They were twelve and thirteen." I looked him directly in the eye. "She should have shot them dead. But she didn't."

Mr. Mickleson stared at me.

"One fired his rifle and hit her." I took a deep breath. "They're both dead now."

He nodded. "And…Ella?"

"We had a chopper there in twenty minutes…"

"*Some guy,* right?"

I nodded. He didn't need to know it all. The blood. The Jeep. The medic. Bleeding out and dying on the floor of the King Bee. The butterflies. "She didn't make it back."

A bit of the stiffness went out of his spine. He was a powerful man. On one of the most powerful streets in the world. He knew people. He knew the levers to pull and the buttons to push in Congress. At the White House. At the State Department. Yet he could not save his daughter.

Of course, neither could I.

We finished our lunch in silence.

The waiter came for our plates.

"I'll have another," he said.

Moments later, a third Martini was placed in front of him.

"Do you mind if I ask?"

"No. What?"

"Were you involved?"

I closed my eyes. I shook my head. "No."

~ ~ ~

Home

I sat out back by the pool. The water glowed blue in the night. I looked up at the few stars I could see through the LA haze. It was late, after midnight, when United got me home from Washington DC.

Behind me, a door opened, then closed quietly.

"Are you going to stay out here all night?" Elaine asked. I recognized her voice without looking, of course.

I shrugged my shoulders.

"Are you drunk?"

"No, but maybe I should be."

"Mmmm, maybe."

She came over, gripped my shoulders and gently massaged them.

"I didn't have anywhere else to go."

"Shhh…You own the place, remember?"

It was Stitch's home in Beverly Hills.

"Oh, yeah. I keep forgetting."

"You want it back?"

I shook my head. "No, you keep it."

"Okay."

I closed my eyes and let my head lean back.

"Did you take care of your business back east?"

I opened my eyes. "How do you know?"

"Sparks stopped by the studio." She smiled. "Who's the little guy?"

"Father Bob."

"Didn't really picture him as the religious type."

"Might not be anymore."

"Well, I fixed them up, and now they're living the dream at the Beverly Hills Hotel."

She came around and sat down beside me. She leaned her head back and looked up at the sky.

I sighed. "I'm so tired."

"Jet lag?"

"I haven't slept in days." I closed my eyes.

She took my hand and held it. "It is the courage to continue that counts."

I felt my head nodding slowly, then drifted off to sleep.

~~~

Thank you for reading my story.

About M.T. Bass

M.T. Bass lives, writes, flies, and plays music in Mudcat Falls, USA.

www.MTBass.net

Available in Paperback & eBook

Hollywood, 1950 — Former P-51 fighter pilot A. Gavin Byrd is on location for a movie shoot, when he gets a call from the police that his older brother, a prominent Beverly Hills plastic surgeon, has been found dead on his boat. The Lieutenant in charge of the investigation is ready to close the case as a suicide from the start, but "Hawk" doesn't buy it and decides to find out what really happened for himself.

With help from a former starlet ex-girlfriend, a friendly police sergeant whose life was saved in the war by his brother and a nosy Los Angeles Times reporter, Hawk's search for the truth takes him through cross-fire, dog fights and mine fields in Hollywood, Beverly Hills, Burbank and Las Vegas, and leads him into some of the darker corners of his brother's patient files and private life that he never knew existed.

www.MTBass.net

Available in Paperback, eBook & Audiobook

She was one in a million…and the day I met her I should have bought a lottery ticket instead.

Griffith Crowe, the "fixer" for a Chicago law firm, falls for his current assignment, Helena Nicholson, the beautiful heir of a Tech Sector venture capitalist who perished in a helicopter crash leaving her half a billion dollars, a Learjet 31, and unsavory suspicions about her father's death. As he investigates, the ex-Navy SEAL crosses swords with Helena's step-brother, the Pentagon's Highlands Forum, and an All-Star bad guy somebody has hired to stop him. When Griff finds himself on the wrong side of an arrest warrant he wonders: Is he a player or being played?

Lawyers and Lovers and Guns…*Oh, my!*

www.MTBass.net

Available in Paperback, eBook & Audiobook

Artificial Intelligence? *Fuhgeddaboudit!*

Artificial Evil has a name…*Munchausen.*

When androids are reprogrammed into hit men, detectives of the Artificial Crimes Unit repo the AnSub and track down the hackers. Partners Jake and EC's case of an "extra-judicial" divorce settlement takes a nasty turn with DNA from a hundred-year-old murder in Boston and a signature that harkens back to the very first serial killer ever in London.

www.MTBass.net

Available in Paperback & eBook

It was the case of a lifetime…but then it went sideways on her. The serial killer Maddie put behind bars might have been crazy but it turns out he was innocent, and now she finds herself hunting robot killers in the Artificial Crimes Unit. Worse yet, she's partnered up with Jake, her former lover.

When androids are hacked and reprogrammed into hit men, Maddie and Jake investigate and track down the hackers. But now, an evil genius is using droids to recreate the infamous Jack the Ripper murders.

www.MTBass.net

Available in Paperback & eBook

Now unleashed, the "Baron" is resurrecting history's notorious serial killers, giving them a second life in the bodies of hacked and reprogrammed Personal Assistant Androids, then turning them loose to terrorize the city. While detectives Jake and Maddie of the police department's Artificial Crimes Unit scramble to stop the carnage with the Baron's arrest, the cyberpunk head of the Counter IT Section, Q, struggles to de-encrypt his mad scheme to infect world data centers with a virus that represents a collective cyber unconsciousness of evil.

Artificial Intelligence? *Fuhgeddaboudit!*

Artificial Evil has a name…*Munchausen*

www.MTBass.net

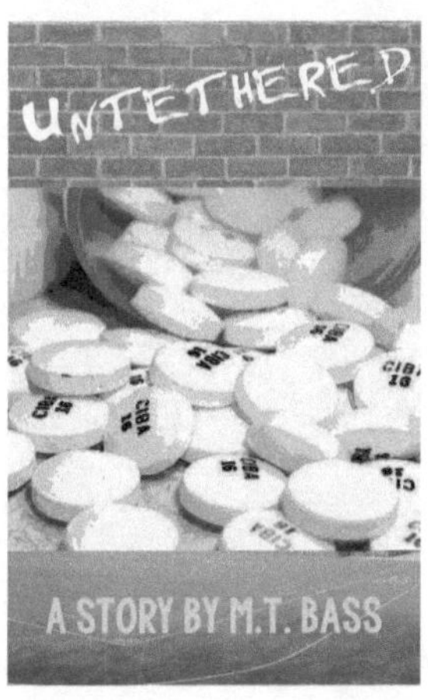

Available in eBook

At District High School #6241, Connor wants only to get close to Liz, the cheerleader whose locker is just across the hall, and forget the suicide of his father in jail, but his family's dark past and a rebellious nature force him to the fringes of student social circles and into an unlikely alliance to fight back against a tyranny of conformity.

www.MTBass.net

Available in Paperback & eBook

People ask me where I get the ideas for my books. In this case, I recall reading about Alaska bush pilots for fun. I must have watched *Animal House* and *Treasure of the Sierra Madre* around that time and…a few months later—Eureka! The words for the prologue and first chapter just started spilling out of my head. ("Clean up on aisle five.")

Seriously, what could go wrong? *Love & Betrayal…Murder & Mayhem…Friendship & Double-Crossing Partners in Pursuit of Buried Treasure…*

www.MTBass.net

Available in eBook

*Lodging — bending of the stalk of a plant (stalk lodging)
or the entire plant (root lodging)*

While World War II engulfs every nation on the globe, Rebecca and her high school friend Sarah can only dream of escaping a dreary, wind-blown existence in western Kansas, until their boring, stodgy old hometown fills with handsome young men learning to fly Army Air Corps bombers known as Liberators, and their lives are suddenly filled with temptation and, perhaps, true love.

www.MTBass.net

Available in Paperback & eBook

Kansas City, 1965 — Y.T. Erp, Jr. can't wait to leave for college at the University of California, Berkeley to escape not only the work, but especially all the phlegm-brained idiots at his father's aerospace company. Leaving behind a pregnant auburn-haired cheerleader, a sensuous red-headed siren plotting to usurp his familial ties, and his two best friends—one who ends up in Vietnam and the other in the Weather Underground—his "trip" on the wild side of the Generation Gap takes him from the psychedelic scene of Haight-Ashbury to the F.B.I.'s Ten Most Wanted list. Meanwhile, his father is consumed by the task of managing his unmanageable corporate team in the quest to help fulfill a President's challenge to "land a man on the moon."

www.MTBass.net

Available in eBook

Cleveland, 1977 — Grappling with a foreign policy crisis, the U.S. Government targets a hapless rock-'n'-roller as a Russian spy in a classic case of mistaken identity for an innocent, 'Wrong Man' hero…or *is he?*

Think of an unholy fictional union between the Rolling Stones and Alfred Hitchcock's *North by Northwest.*

Unlike any novel you have ever read, this one has a soundtrack. After all, a story whose characters are musicians should have…well…*music.* Right?

www.MTBass.net